A desparate act

"Please!" the white-haired cop said. "Don't do it. The negotiator will be here in just a second and she'll know just what to say. Just wait a little while . . . please!"

Harry looked out at the world, at the tops of the buildings, the little people down below, connected by so many things, disconnected by so few. Subject to disease and war, one hand reaching for the stars, the other slinking back to the darkest cave. And all this time, he'd thought it had somehow all made sense, that he could figure it out.

But he was wrong.

"When you're right, you're right," he said to himself. "It doesn't make any sense. Not one bit."

He turned to look at the cop. "I'm really sorry about this," he said.

The cop lunged forward to grab him, but Harry smiled, shrugged, and moved his feet over the ledge.

Briefly, Harry felt weightless, just like he had so many years ago, trapped in his father's arms at the top of an amusement-park ride. There'd be no parachute this time, though. His stomach lurched. Everything spun. He was expecting to fly, but he wasn't flying. He was falling.

It would all be over i

The TimeTripper series

TIME TRIPPER

BOOK FOUR: FUTUREIMPERFECT

STEFAN PETRUCHA

razOr
bill

TimeTripper 4: FutureImperfect

RAZORBILL

Published by the Penguin Group
Penguin Young Readers Group
345 Hudson Street, New York, New York 10014, U.S.A.
Penguin Group (USA) Inc., 375 Hudson Street, New York, New York
10014, U.S.A.
Penguin Group (Canada), 90 Eglinton Avenue East, Suite 700, Toronto,
Ontario, Canada M4P 2Y3 (a division of Pearson Penguin Canada Inc.)
Penguin Books Ltd, 80 Strand, London WC2R 0RL, England
Penguin Ireland, 25 St Stephen's Green, Dublin 2, Ireland
(a division of Penguin Books Ltd)
Penguin Group (Australia), 250 Camberwell Road, Camberwell, Victoria
3124, Australia (a division of Pearson Australia Group Pty Ltd)
Penguin Books India Pvt Ltd, 11 Community Centre, Panchsheel Park,
New Delhi – 110 017, India
Penguin Group (NZ), Cnr Airborne and Rosedale Roads, Albany,
Auckland 1310, New Zealand (a division of Pearson New Zealand Ltd)
Penguin Books (South Africa) (Pty) Ltd, 24 Sturdee Avenue,
Rosebank, Johannesburg 2196, South Africa

Penguin Books Ltd, Registered Offices: 80 Strand, London WC2R 0RL,
England

10 9 8 7 6 5 4 3 2 1

Library of Congress Cataloging-in-Publication Data is available

Printed in the United States of America

Is it sublime that each moment of time

If predestined, makes free will a sham?

Or is life a feast where all manner of beast

Can refuse their consent to the plan?

Though the issue confounds every madman and clown

I prefer to lose track of the rules.

For even the Fates throw their thread to the wind

When they capture the eye of a Fool.

—SIARA WARNER, 10TH GRADE

1. *Hey, Harry, why don't you kill yourself? Come on, it'll be fun! Just do it!*

It was the Quirk-shard talking, the one that kept trying to get him to commit suicide. He'd gotten it in A-Time, the timeless state Harry could enter where past, present, and future existed side by side. Animal-like bundles of events, Quirks wandered the terrain trying to happen. While Harry had been fighting one, he'd gotten stuck with a claw. Ever since, it'd been trying to get him to jump off a tall building. Here in linear time, it appeared as that little voice in the back of his head.

Harry Keller laughed, thinking that, at least here in Windfree Sanitarium, it could scream all it wanted with no results.

Just the same way Harry screamed. All angst. No payoff.

"Sorry," Harry said to the voice. "Door's bolted. Guard's outside."

Damn, the Quirk-shard said.

Other thoughts skittered around his head looking for places to hide, like cockroaches in the kitchen when the lights come on.

Can't get there from here.

Hi, Harry, we're the insides of your eyelids!

Elijah isn't real.

1

I'm afraid there's been a misunderstanding.

Alligator, alligator, humpback whale.

Slowly, Harry opened his eyes. They felt dry, painfully dry, like his throat. Thick eye-gunk clung to his lids and eyelashes. It was a side effect of the medication they kept plunging into him every few hours. They just came in, rolled him to the side, and jabbed the needle through a little canvas patch in the straitjacket that flipped open on his arm, like the butt-flap on a toddler's pajamas.

His hands were wrapped around his body by the jacket, so he couldn't lift or clench them. All he could do, really, was sort of swish them up and down at the wrist, in a vague scratching motion. He moved his head. His neck hurt at the base of his skull. Another side effect, or had he just been in the same position for too long?

What with all the meds they were giving him, being locked up and insane shouldn't feel so bad. He should be docile. His hallucination and paranoia should be receding. Maybe they were. He wasn't screaming anymore.

Why haven't the meds worked? Why can't I calm down? Why am I still conscious, if you can call it that?

Apparently even the expert tweaking of his seratonin and dopamine levels hadn't extinguished the nagging sensation in the back of his mind that there was something terribly, terribly important he was supposed to be doing.

Shutting off the lights in the loft? No.

Finishing some homework? Nope.

Turning off a burner on the stove? No.

Saving Siara's life and stopping the evil plans of her boyfriend, Jeremy Gronson, who was manipulating A-Time to cause death and general mayhem?

Oh yeah. That was it.

"Let me out! Let me out! He'll kill you all!" Harry screeched.

His throat ached from the effort, but apparently he wasn't as tired as he thought. He strained, trying to pull himself to a standing position. When he couldn't, he let himself slump against the wall and huffed a few times as if that might calm him.

Harry blinked to try to loosen some of the gunk, then looked around—same old, same old: white padded walls, floor and ceiling. Everything looked like the surface of a bare mattress, complete with strange stains. Even the door had padding. It also had that little window toward the top—the one the interns and doctors solemnly peered through now and again to see if he was still alive, or if he'd died or turned into a newt or something.

If I could just shrink my body down to the right size, I could slip through that window . . . , Harry thought. *Or better yet, if only I could just make the rest of the world larger . . .*

At least he was forming sentences. That was an

3

improvement from when his aunt had visited. He remembered hearing her voice, angry in the hall. She kept shouting in that loud actress voice of hers, until finally the door clicked open and the stale air from the hall mixed with the equally stale air in the room.

She came in, knelt beside him, pushed the hair out of his eyes, and pressed her palm flat against his forehead as if checking for a fever. He remembered how much her hand felt like a mother's hand, maybe even his own mother's, though he couldn't remember her at all.

Why shouldn't it? They were sisters. There was something familiar in her face, maybe something he recognized from the photos his father kept in the old apartment. Insanity ran in the family. His aunt was never the most stable person either—but it was okay for an actress to be flighty.

She'd looked at him, tears in her eyes, and said, "Why don't you just *pretend* to be sane? Why not just pretend? It's all anyone ever does, really. It's all that sanity is."

Easy for her to say, but it was a game Harry had never learned to master.

He tried to answer, to tell her he'd try, but all he could make was a gurgling sound. He couldn't even talk, let alone pretend, and he certainly couldn't explain how deep-down broken he felt. A busted hand

4

you can explain—you can say, See? I can't move my fingers so I can't pick up that cup of coffee—and most people understand that.

But a brain? How do you get that across? Sure, everyone has brain farts, where they forget a word or go off on some weird tangent for a bit, but how do you explain getting stuck on that weird tangent, getting lost and having no idea which way is home? It was like being trapped half asleep, stuck in neutral like it was cement, totally not sure which side had the dreams and which side the world.

Aunt Shirley's hand went away and she left. Slowly, the warm spot on his forehead where her palm had touched went cold. Soon it was as though she'd never been there at all. After they gave him his next shots, he was no longer sure if she'd been there at all or if he'd just imagined it.

Imagined it. Yeah, like the girl he'd fallen so quickly in love with. Elijah, who did not exist, whom he'd kissed, who was just some part of himself. How lame was that?

Maybe he'd imagined Siara and Jeremy, too—and Todd and the Quirks, the Glitch, the whole ball of wax. Maybe he'd imagined his father, his whole life. Maybe he'd imagined himself. It'd be kind of a relief at this point. But no, that nagging sense of danger wouldn't let him go. It was worse than the voice of the Quirk-shard.

I have to get out of here! I have to go save Siara! I have to save the world.

Even if he could spell it out for his aunt or the doctors, they'd just double his meds

. . . throw the door and lock away the key.

He noticed something lying flat on the floor in the center of the room. It was rectangular, dirty green. He blinked and tried to get it into focus. As he managed to clear the last of the eye-gunk away, he saw what it was.

A book.

What the hell?

There was a book lying on the floor in the center of his padded cell. Hardcover, no less. What would a book be doing there? Could his aunt have left it? No. He certainly didn't remember her leaving anything, and the doctors had been in here at least once since she'd left. Was there some library here that delivered? Nah. Books couldn't possibly be allowed in padded cells, could they? TV, maybe, but a book? That'd just be torture for someone in a straitjacket. Not as bad as leaving a back-scratcher, but still.

Harry stared at it. The muscles in his forehead ached as he furrowed his brow. At least it seemed to bring his attention back into the room, away from the beehive buzz in his brain. It was kind of like a toy. Something to play with. He twisted his head sideways trying to make some sense of it.

Was it real? It looked real.

Could it be any good? It looked like it might be a good book.

No, it *felt* like it might be a good book.

Can't judge a book by its cover, or the world by the way you feel.

Hm. That was almost coherent.

Curious, but a little afraid, he put his feet out and pulled, so that his butt moved along the bumpy surface. His straitjacket, scraping along the floor, made a loud noise, so he cast a nervous glance at the door's little window. If the book didn't belong here and someone saw it, they might try to take it away.

Slowing, he managed to inch closer more quietly. Soon he saw some letters on the cover, not just printed, but embossed in gold type. They formed just one word. Nothing on the spine, nothing else on the cover, just that one word—but he couldn't quite make out what it was.

He shimmied closer. A strange excitement got the better of him and he lost his balance and landed hard on his cheek. The cloth on the floor was like sandpaper, scraping as he rubbed against it.

Rather than waste time trying to sit up, he gritted his teeth and bent and unbent at the waist, crawling like a human caterpillar. With a sigh of relief, he bumped his forehead against the book's edge, then used his chin to spin it around.

The word on the cover was clear now, inches from his eyes. It said:

HARRY

Well, that was interesting. Now there were two things in here named Harry, him and the book. He was vaguely aware that his thoughts seemed to calm down a bit as he stared at it, vaguely aware he wasn't even quite thinking about Jeremy and Siara anymore. Were the drugs finally kicking in, or was it the book?

Pff. The book. Right. Maybe it was a *magic* book with three wishes in it. More likely it *was* a gift from his aunt, a diary he could write down his crazy thoughts in.

Or maybe not.

He leaned forward and put his nose under the cover, planning to flip it open and have a look at the first page. As he did, he heard a familiar rattle at the door.

Someone was coming in.

Terrified the book would be found, Harry flopped forward, covering it with his chest. As the door opened, he turned his head sideways and saw the black shoes and white pants of one of the interns.

"Now how'd you get yourself in that screwed-up position?"

Harry recognized the voice. It was Jesus, one of the nicer interns. He actually used an alcohol swab to clean Harry's arm before plunging the needle in. He wondered if Jesus sometimes looked in the mirror and said to himself, "What would *I* do?"

But the only thing Harry knew about Jesus was that

he sometimes got massive headaches and took ibuprofen five capsules at a time.

"Time to sit up," Jesus said.

He started to pull Harry into a seated position.

No! He'll see the book, he'll take it away!

Harry was lifted like a doll and. The butt-flap on his arm opened. He felt the cool of the alcohol swab, the queasy prick of the needle.

"There," Jesus said. "Be easier if you'd take the pills."

But I don't want to!

It dawned on him he could have said so. The words were right there, on the tip of his tongue.

Jesus seemed to sense it. He eyed Harry, and said, "Something you want to say?"

But Harry chose not to answer. He just grunted, but this time it was on purpose. Jesus shrugged and left, sealing the door behind him.

And he hadn't taken the book. Hadn't seemed to notice it. How could he miss it? It was green and square while everything else in the room was white and puffy, like a pillow.

Was it really there?

Harry wriggled close to it again and this time managed to flip it open with the tip of his foot.

The first page was nearly as blank as the cover, but in the center were more words. He flopped down to read them. They said:

HARRY, COME AND PLAY WITH ME.

Harry reared. It felt like the book was talking to him, but that was crazy.

At least I'm dressed for it.

He felt the drugs swarm in his system, shook his head to try to clear it.

Why does this feel so familiar?

Warmth traveled up his arm from the site of the injection. He felt the cacophony in his mind subside, a sensation that should have brought relief, but as he stared at those six black words on the pure white page, his heart beat faster until his chest felt like a balloon pumped too full of air.

Not just any balloon. A clown balloon.

That was it. The feeling was the same he had whenever that strange clown balloon appeared.

He'd thought the image and the feeling were gone forever after he'd seen the clown statue at the amusement park, after he'd remembered it was just a childhood memory, warped and twisted by time.

He looked around. The clown balloon wasn't here, but the feeling increased a thousandfold, as if it were trying to break through some invisible wall in Harry's soul, to take over his whole body, drive him out, make *him* the hallucination.

Then again, maybe it was just the drugs kicking in.

Harry looked back at the page. Full of trepidation, he spoke his first coherent sentence in days.

"What if I don't want to come and play with you?" Then, using his chin, he flipped to the next page, which read:

YOU DON'T HAVE A CHOICE.

Mystified, terrified, horrified, Harry kicked the book away. His face shook, his body shivered as he tried to get the image of the words out of his head.

Take it away! Take it away!

He fell, crawled, moving like a mad insect, trying to put as much distance between himself and the book as possible. He rubbed his face so quickly against the floor, his cheek bled, but he didn't care. Finally, he managed to get his back against the far wall, then, panting and frightened, proceeded to try to press himself into it.

He closed his eyes. What did it mean? What could it mean? The book was talking to him, directly to him.

It wasn't like the clown balloon or any of the mad A-Time images. This just felt real, in a sickly dizzying kind of way. Like he just couldn't tell anymore, like he just couldn't tell one world from another, or any world from a stray thought. He was lost and getting more lost, tumbling into a black abyss where he would be forever insane, where there'd be no way, anymore, ever, to tell what was real and what was not.

This was crazy, oh yes. This was it: the final collapse of his mind, where he'd taken the plunge into eternal elsewhere.

It felt worse than finding out Elijah wasn't real. Worse than knowing Siara was at the mercy of Jeremy, because it felt like it was making all that and more totally unreal.

Please God, no more, no more. No more hallucinations.

And then, just as he thought he'd reached the limit of what his senses could bear, there came a titanic rumbling, the sound of mortar, rock, and wood straining under some greater power. He felt the vibrations run through his body as the walls began to shake. He opened his eyes in time to see the thick padding that covered the room tear, exposing the white fluffs of stuffing inside.

The top half of the room lifted free. Above and beyond, Harry could see the sky and the clouds above Windfree Sanitarium. Where the world had just been the tiny room, now it headed off into forever.

Most horrifying of all, the piece of building that had just been torn free from its foundation hovered in the air, held by a giant, white-gloved hand.

And there, impossibly huge, stood the clown from the balloon, his hair an orange forest, his white face a vast, featureless desert, the red and blue of his eyes and mouth glowing brighter than any colors Harry had ever seen.

And when it opened its mouth, showed its mountainous teeth and writhing, oceanic tongue, and spoke, the force of its deep voice felt as though it were ripping a hole in Harry's head.

I SAID, COME OUT AND PLAY WITH ME!

Son of a bitch, Harry thought. *Everything's real.*

2. Her red eyes had black streaks around them, where a mask of Halloween greasepaint had been quickly wiped away. She smelled of soot and smoke. Her brunette hair, mussed, had gray bits of ash woven into it. She'd been in the fire that had almost wiped out Robert A. Wilson High School's entire senior class. That was just last night, but here she was, in school, in Emeril Tippicks's tiny office, sitting in a small blue plastic chair, her lean form folded fetally.

Why? What had possessed her to come to school today? Moreover, what had possessed her, as Tippicks had been told, to run into the blazing warehouse and save Harry Keller's life?

Tippicks didn't ask out loud, but he didn't have to. She coughed, scrunched her face, swiped a dry, plum-dyed clump of hair from her forehead, and said, "I have to talk to you about Harry."

Tippicks had been up since three because of the fire, fielding calls, filling out forms. Now he was in a death match with a vengeful headache. Sleepless and disheveled, he knew he looked more like a balding, gray-haired turkey than a role model, but he wanted to help.

So he leaned forward and immediately knocked over a mug crammed with pens and pencils. Some flew into his lap, others rolled helter-skelter across the desk, while a few clattered to the linoleum floor. The thin plastic sounds echoed in his head like slamming doors.

"It must be hard," Tippicks said hoarsely as he scrambled to scoop up the rolling pens within his reach. He stuffed a handful back in the mug, leaving little blue and red marks on his palm. "We're all very worried and disappointed about what happened to Harry. The trauma of the fire must have tipped him over the edge."

Not only that, but Tippicks knew he'd been personally stupid about the whole thing. He'd protected Keller too much, ignored obvious signs, made a mistake in helping him stay off the antipsychotic meds. He had actually covered for the boy as he hid in a locker in the girls' gym.

Why?

An image of Tippicks's father in a padded cell in Windfree flashed into his mind, making his head pound all the more. He tried to distract himself by scooping more pens into his hands.

The girl crossed her arms and buried her hands between her knees. "It's not that. Not just that, anyway."

Tippicks lowered more pens into the mug. "Well, what then?"

Disdain wrinkled her young face. "Don't you want to ask if I knew whether or not he was taking any drugs?"

Tippicks clamped his eyes shut. As if he wasn't feeling guilty enough, he remembered he'd rifled through this girl's book-bag yesterday, found a stash of K, then doubted her story—which turned out to be true—that it had been planted on her.

He shrugged. "No. I just want to know whatever it is you want to tell me."

"Well, he wasn't. Harry never used any drugs. Not one. Do you believe me?"

Tippicks's brow furrowed. "Yes."

She fell into a troubled silence, so he reached for his phone.

"You might find it easier talking to another counselor."

"No," she said. "It has to be you. Harry trusted *you*."

"But clearly you don't. I understand. It's okay, but—"

"I . . . I have to try."

Tippicks withdrew his hand from the phone and leaned back in his chair. It creaked as it tilted back, and a pencil on his lap rolled off onto the floor. When he winced, Siara stifled a snicker.

He smiled. He opened up his hands. "I'm all ears."

"You won't tell his doctors? Is anything I say here . . . you know, private?"

"I won't tell anyone," Tippicks said. "As long as it doesn't involve murder."

"And if it does?"

His smile faded. Out of the corner of his eye he saw another pencil rolling. He could have caught it easily, but let it drop.

"What are you talking about?"

"Harry thought someone was trying to drive him crazy or kill him," she said. She looked around nervously, like she was betraying a trust, but eventually locked eyes with Tippicks. "He thought they started the fire at the warehouse just to get to him."

Tippicks felt his body tense. Something gurgled in his stomach. Perhaps it was his long-dormant acid reflux coming back for a visit. He tried not to let the pain show.

"Harry's mind works quickly. Too quickly for his own good. They say he's been delusional . . . ," he began.

But she cut him off with a shake of her head that said simply, *No. You don't get it.*

"It works faster than that," she said. "Faster than anything. It works so fast you can break it just by giving it a little shove. Remember the shooting? Harry thought someone was trying to make Todd Penderwhistle kill Jeremy Gronson, then kill himself. He thought somebody was trying to turn Melody Glissando into a murderer. . . ."

She was talking too fast, so Tippicks raised his hand to try to slow her down, make her think more rationally.

But her words came out in a flood.

"And he stopped them. He did the right things at the right time, and he stopped them. Then he figured out that whoever it was who did all this was after him now. He had a new girlfriend, Elijah. I thought it was her, but it turns out no one at school ever even saw her except Harry. I'm starting to think he just hallucinated her, or someone made him hallucinate her, just to drive him crazy."

Tippicks pressed his fingers into his temples and rubbed. The poor girl was tired, upset. Keller could be persuasive. He'd probably talked her into sharing his delusions, and now she didn't know which end was up anymore.

He tried to make his crackly voice sound gentle: "He's your friend, so naturally you believed him when he told you these things, yes?"

She gave him that derisive, impatient head shake again. "Hell no, I thought he was nuts. But then he showed me. In the auditorium, when Todd fired at Jeremy, Jeremy tripped on some chairs and the bullet missed him. Harry arranged those chairs."

Tippicks kept rubbing. "I remember. It was in the security report."

"He can see the future and rearrange it."

The burning stomach acid lapped up into his throat. "Excuse me?"

As if gesticulating would make things clearer, she flared and waved her fingers as she spoke. "He can make it so that things that were going to happen, don't. Or sometimes he can make it so that things that were never going to happen, do."

The image of his father in Windfree, babbling nonsense, again flashed in Tippicks's head.

"How . . . how does Harry change the future?" he said. His voice was weak, his eyes closed.

Her voice was tinged with regret. "You just think he's crazy, and now you think *I'm* crazy, too, don't you?"

Tippicks shrugged and shook his head. He opened his eyes and offered a weary smile. "No. I think we're all tired. As for crazy, some of my favorite people are crazy. I only asked a question: How? How does Harry change the future?"

He saw the girl swallow hard.

"He thinks the part of his brain that organizes reality into linear time was damaged by the trauma of losing his father."

Tippicks's brow didn't just furrow; it knotted. Something old and dark was dragged out from inside of him, and he was too weak to stop it.

"Go on."

"His brain takes him to this place where he can see

the past, the present, and the future all at the same time in, like, these trails. The past is hard, but the future is like clay, and he can change it. He calls it A-Time."

Tippicks couldn't keep himself from asking, "And you say you've seen it?"

She stared at him, seeing something new in his face that made her speak more confidently. "Yes. He took me there. I'm not sure how. He did it just by talking to me. I was dizzy the whole time, but I saw these . . . these *beasts* there."

"That try to become part of the trails. That try to . . . happen," Tippicks said numbly.

It was Siara's turn to scrunch her brow. "Yeah. Exactly. Did Harry already tell you?"

Tippicks blank expression ruffled to life. "No, no. I . . . I just guessed."

He was lying, and it was clear from the single eyebrow she raised that she didn't buy it. After a pause, she continued, probably figuring in for a penny, in for a pound.

"Harry thinks there's someone else in A-Time, too. He called him the Daemon. And now Harry's . . . now he's really crazy and he's locked up and all alone, and I'm afraid something even worse is going to happen to him. I thought maybe you could help him, tell someone who might give him a chance to prove what he's saying is true."

Tippicks stared at her, unable to move. He saw her

shrink, fold back into her near-fetal position. After a too-long silence, a disheartened Siara Warner, eyes downcast, stood to leave.

"Maybe I shouldn't have come."

"No," Tippicks said. "Please. I just need some time to think. I want to help, but I'm not sure . . . I'm not sure where to begin. Give me some time. I'll try to live up to your trust."

She scanned him, exhaled through her nose, and slipped out of his office into the noise-filled hall.

As he saw the rush of student bodies file past his open door, Tippicks mulled her words and the guileless sincerity of her tone.

A broken brain that saw through time. Monsters that ate fate. A place of infinite possibility that could be molded with your hands. It was almost exactly, word for word, what his father had talked about when they locked him up forever.

Tippicks rose and closed the office door. He massaged his brow long and hard, squeezed the bridge of his nose between his thumb and forefinger, all the while remembering how his father had begged him to believe, and how he couldn't.

It was then that Emeril Tippicks decided he would do yet another stupid thing. He would pay a visit to Harry Keller in his padded cell just as soon as possible.

But first, he had to find some aspirin and clean up the rest of these pens.

3. Mother's voice, sweet as honey, came floating down the hall all the way into Jeremy's room.

"Jeremy, is our tea ready yet?"

Jeremy Gronson shook his head, even though he knew she couldn't see him.

"It's steeping. I've got the timer on," he called.

"Exactly four and a half minutes?" his father chimed in distractedly. He could hear the old man ruffle the pages of the *Wall Street Journal* as he spoke.

"Exactly, Dad," he answered. "Four and a half minutes."

He shut the door, even though he knew most of the sound would still carry.

Shirtless, Jeremy felt the cool air in his room, the warm carpet beneath his bare feet. He bent forward, exhaling, pushing his palms to the floor, legs straight, knees not locked, back flat. A few bones in his spine loosened and clicked into place. His taut muscles burned deliciously. He inhaled slowly, exhaled even slower.

After rolling up out of the stretch, one vertebra at a time, he turned toward a hand-carved ivory chess set on the table next to his desk and stared at the pieces.

They were set up to reproduce a game he'd played with Harry Keller the other day, a game Keller would have won if the idiot had bothered staying to finish.

Since then, Jeremy had played the moves over and over, dozens of times, on the board, on the computer, in his head, trying to figure out where he went wrong. But he couldn't. Keller's moves were stupid, ridiculous. They seemed to defy logic. But they worked.

Since they worked, all that meant was that they were somehow logical, but that Jeremy didn't see the logic yet. In the end, everything made sense, everything had some kind of order. Everything. It just had to. And Jeremy Gronson just had to understand everything.

Seeing a different tack, he lifted the rook. The small ebon tower caught bits of light from the recessed bulbs in the ceiling. He held it awhile, pondering, then set it down in a new spot. Now the patterns of the pieces looked familiar, ordered. Everything was in its place again. Everything perfect. He knew just what to do next.

He imagined the game playing out, saw his pieces as if they were his football teammates: moving across the field, pushing through the frail defense, passing him the ball, so he could run and run until . . .

"Argh!"

Jeremy swatted at the pieces, sweeping as many as

he could into the air. The black king shattered a water glass. A white pawn made a small indentation in the wall.

He still lost. Through some insane accident, he still lost.

But then again, there were no accidents.

"Jeremy?" Mother said, her voice muffled by the door. "Everything all right in there?"

"Yes. Fine."

"Are you still thinking about that girl?" Father asked loudly. Even through the door and the wall, Father had heard the tension in his voice. Father was always hearing things in his voice. He just never understood what they were about. Of course he was thinking about the girl, but not for the stupid hormonal reasons Father suspected.

He shook his head. "No, Dad. I'm not thinking about the girl."

He imagined the board again in his mind, piece by piece, move by move. Then he imagined himself swatting that away as well.

It was a trick, it had to be—just a trick. Maybe it was one of the tricks the Obscure Masters would reveal when he finished his initiation. Just as soon as he won the last game.

Far off, a timer beeped.

"Jeremy! Our tea's ready!"

"I know, Dad. I know."

"Can't have servants every day, Jay."

Jeremy winced. He hated when father called him Jay.

"You scare the crap out me, Siara," her dad said as the evening sky, visible through the window behind him, swelled over the city.

Reality bites, she thought. They sat in the barely-eat-in kitchen at a table that had been too small for the three of them for years, she steadily meeting his totally glaring eyes.

She tried to get through to him one more time. "I had to go into the fire to save Harry. And Jeremy, the boyfriend you were pushing me to stay with, took me to that party in the first place. As for the riot, well . . . the charges were dropped."

Forget it. It was useless. She didn't believe any of it herself. She blasted some air through her curled lower lip, up at the plum-red strands on her forehead. They weren't in her eyes; she just did it out of nervousness and because she was kind of hoping it might look cute enough to lower the Dad Anger Quotient.

It didn't.

"The charges were dropped," he repeated slowly. "How'd we get here, exactly?"

She gave him a sheepish grin. "Take a left at adolescence?"

Even her most humble, self-deprecating humor didn't break through. He didn't laugh.

"You're grounded for a month. Really, not like last time. I'm putting locks on your windows so there'll be no more sneaking out via the fire escape."

"But—"

"You go to school, you come home. You do your homework, you go to bed, you wake up, you go to school. Repeat for thirty days. On weekends maybe we'll walk you around the block a few times for exercise, but that's it."

"Can I . . . can I go see Harry?"

"No."

Siara's indignation rose with her voice. "He's all alone. He doesn't have much family. He's my . . . friend. Shouldn't I stick by him? Aren't you the one who told me I should always do what I think is right?"

Her father shook his head. "I misspoke. What I meant to say was that you should always do what *I* think is right."

He was so pissed.

This is why it's so hard to trust your parents with the secrets of time and space.

Feeling like a rat grasping at straws, she asked, "Does Mom know you're doing this?"

He blinked and sighed. "Don't go complaining to her, Siara. Just don't. She's got enough on her mind. The demo's tomorrow night."

Demo?

As if her home had suddenly appeared out of

30

nowhere, Siara looked around at the dirty dishes in the sink, the scattered papers on the counter, and the dust gathering at the edges of the flower-patterned linoleum floor. The apartment was a mess, and she remembered for the first time why.

Her mother hadn't been around much lately.

"Oh yeah. The demo," Siara said, wincing. A wet blanket of guilt briefly smothered thoughts of Harry. Peroxisome Inc. was coming to RAW to show off "H to O," their new fuel cell engine. Mom was a broom-pushing, coffee-getting assistant at the lab, but she'd been put in charge of the demo. It was her big break. She was also excited about showing off her daughter to the company bigwigs, so excited she didn't even hear Siara wail about the major embarrassment factor when she insisted Siara wear a gross business suit—"Peroxisome code!"—and help with the catering.

"Yeah. That," Dad said slowly.

It was hopeless. No way out. "Fine. Okay. I'll take the grounding. I'll help you put locks on the windows, and of course I'll support Mom. I'll even go to counseling, whatever . . . but, Dad, I've *got* to see Harry. I'd go myself, but the bus ride's three hours and . . ."

Her father raised a single eyebrow, exactly the same way Siara herself did when something totally, utterly pointless was going on. If that eyebrow had been a sword it would have cut her in two.

Defeated, she slid her chair away from the too-small

table and walked by the overloaded sink, vaguely thinking she should pitch in and clean up. She lived here, too, after all. Sort of.

More and more often it felt like she didn't. It just didn't feel like her apartment, or her planet anymore. A-Time had changed all that. Harry had. A more exciting world was waiting out there, full of adventures, mistakes, and victories, both pointless and profound. Siara wanted to run into it full-tilt, but her feet kept getting stuck here, where she was still considered a child.

Her father didn't know any of that. To him, she only looked troubled. It wasn't his fault, so just before exiting the kitchen, she turned back and said, "Sorry."

He exhaled and finally lowered the damn eyebrow. "I know. Look, let's both try to pretend we're sane for your mother's sake, just until after tomorrow night. Then . . . maybe I will drive you to see your friend. Past that, RAW . . . maybe it's too much pressure for you poets. Maybe we should talk about alternatives."

Her mouth dropped open. He'd said time and time again that he wanted her to be a lawyer or a doctor, and RAW, supposedly one of the best high schools in the country, was phase one of that plan. Being offered a chance to switch schools should be a big exhale, a sigh of relief, but right now it didn't feel like that at all. It felt like a failure.

She slunk out of the kitchen, feeling her father stare

at her back. As her eyes greeted the dark of the hallway, an image of Harry flashed in her mind; he in the back of an ambulance, strapped to a gurney, grunting, straining, mouth open so wide it threatened to tear the corners of his lips. Everything about him screamed that he'd figured out something important, something so horribly important it had driven him completely insane.

She worried it was just reality he'd figured out, that understanding reality would drive anyone insane. But it seemed more important than that. Would she get to him in time to find out what it was? Time. Ha. Her old poem, the one she was writing when Harry went berserk in the auditorium a few months ago, seemed to cling to her hair.

Pushing the present from six until twelve,
Sisyphus times his own prison

Prison. Like Windfree. What would she do if she got there? Free him? It was terrible to think of him locked up, to imagine him in a straitjacket trying to talk to people who thought he was just delusional. But she couldn't stop thinking about it. The images stuck to her heart as if they were covered with glue. Maybe the meds would have calmed him down enough so that he'd be able to explain things to her.

What could it possibly be like to be caged like that, surrounded by people who couldn't—who *wouldn't*—believe you?

She walked into her room and spotted a plastic Sears bag on her desk. When she upended it, the heavy-duty window locks her father had bought thudded onto her desk.

A little like this?

But her window wasn't locked yet. It was still half-open. A cool late autumn wind wafted in, caressing her face and neck, giving her a chill. Visible above the apartment buildings across the street, the glow of the evening sky beckoned.

What should she do?

Siara had her hands on the window. She was ready to push up, open it all the way, and hit the fire escape. She could take the bus, hitch. She could make it.

I'm coming, Harry!

But the sound of a key in a lock stopped her.

Turning to the hallway, she peeked at the front door to the apartment. A world away, a smartly dressed woman in her mid-forties, who looked like Siara but with carefully coiffed hair, appeared. She carried a briefcase and a well-worn smile. Not seeing Siara in the dim hallway, she paused at the kitchen door and looked in. As she spoke to her husband, the smile remained, but her eyes crinkled.

"Any new crises?" she asked cautiously. "Murder arrest maybe?"

"No," Siara heard her dad answer. "Not yet. And, as I was told, the charges were dropped."

Siara stepped back into that world and gave her mother a little wave. "Hi, Mommy."

Mom's smile widened. It seemed tired but wise. "Are we working on a new crisis?"

"Not intentionally," she lied.

"Not until after my demo tomorrow night, right?" she asked. She stepped up and pushed the plum hair gently back on Siara's head.

"Right," Siara echoed.

"Sweetie," Mom said, "I understand if you want to stay home and rest, but I sure could use you for an hour at the school. It might help you take your mind off things."

"You should go," her father chimed in. "Beats moping around."

"Fine," Siara said. "I'll go. I'm happy to help, Mom."

Her mother kissed her on the forehead. "Let me get some things together. Give me twenty minutes."

Siara eyed her father, who offered her his own, weaker smile, then headed back to her room. Just as she closed her door, she heard him say, "I really think it's time we got a bigger table."

With the door creating the illusion of privacy, she looked at her little room: the pine desk in the corner by the window, loose papers covering the spot her footprint left the last time she snuck out; the short bookshelf with thick white paint that held sundry volumes —an ancient Poe, Tennyson's *Idylls of the King*, some dog-eared Dickinson, an illustrated Rumi, collected Bishop, TS Eliot. Her mother had bought her some Whitman a while back, but so far, he'd just given her a headache.

She thought about seeking some solace there, in the poems, but her mind was still locked on Harry. The longer she left him alone, the more she was sure something bad would happen.

She couldn't get to Harry tonight, no way. Her parents would freak if she went missing again, but maybe she could cut school tomorrow, get a note from Mr. Tippicks. She could take the bus or the train as far as it could go, then cab it or hitchhike. Yeah, like that wasn't suicide. Even then, would there be enough time to get to Windfree and back for the demo?

Maybe.

If only Dree, Jasmine, or Hutch owned a car. Hutch would probably steal one for her, but grand theft auto didn't seem like a good idea either.

The phone rang. Maybe it was one of them calling to get the lowdown. Moving quickly before her parents could answer, and maybe stop the conversation, she grabbed the phone and, without bothering to check the CID, pressed talk.

"Hello?"

"Hi, Siara," a male voice answered. It was slow and uncertain, but she knew who it was.

"Jeremy?"

Did he want to yell at her? He didn't sound angry.

"I'm . . . just checking in. You know, wanted to see if you're all right, that sort of thing."

Wow—he's not thinking we're still together, is he? He couldn't possibly be that dense. How many times do you have to hit a guy with a crowbar before he gets the idea?

Filled with anxious energy, she found it easy to say what she assumed had been implied. "Jeremy, I really don't think we should be seeing each other anymore."

He just laughed. "Yeah. I sort of got that impression when you whacked me upside the head."

Okay, so that's not it.

"Right. Sorry. So . . . how's your head?"

"Bruised. No concussion, though."

"Jeremy, I had to—"

"I know. You had to save Harry Keller. And I had to try to stop you, and if I'd succeeded, he *would* be dead right now, and I'd be wondering if I should've stopped you. So I guess you were right."

"Wow. Jeremy, that's so . . . enlightened. You sure your head's okay?"

"Come on, Siara, have I ever been a bad guy to you?"

"No," she admitted. "Never."

Even Harry had tried to strangle her once. Of course, he was possessed by a Glitch at the time.

"Glad we got that straight. I just wanted to let you know that there are no hard feelings or anything, and I guess I understand why things didn't work out, even though I don't really."

"We're just really different, Jeremy."

"Yeah. That was why I liked you. I thought we had this yin-yang thing going. I always really liked your poem about the clock and that Greek guy, Emphasis."

"That's Sisyphus, Jeremy, but come on. You're the captain of the football team and the chess team. You've got your pick of any girl in the school. You'll get over me."

"Sure, but I figure it'll take a week or so."

Just a week? Siara thought, but she laughed a little into the phone.

"That's how long I'm grounded, anyway," Jeremy said with a weird little chuckle. "It's ridiculous. I'm eighteen, I should be able to do whatever I want, but the folks pay the bills on the Humvee, so I'm only supposed to take it to and from school for the next two weeks. You?"

"A month. I'll probably get time off for good behavior after I help out with my mom's demo, but I just wish——"

"What?"

"No. Never mind."

"Go ahead, tell me."

"No. It's not fair to you," Siara said.

"We're way past fair, Siara. At least let's stay honest. Say it."

"Okay. I really want go see Harry."

There was a brief silence.

"I should've guessed. So why don't you? That part of the grounding?"

"My dad doesn't think I should go see him, especially not before the demo."

"He's right," Jeremy answered flatly

"What? You think Harry's a bad influence, too?"

There was that chuckle again. It sounded strange, almost nerdy, coming from the big jock. "I just think it'd be upsetting. You saw him in the ambulance. He's totally freaked. He'll probably be more stable after he's been on the meds awhile. Isn't that how it works for people like him?"

People like him.

"I know . . . I just . . . Jeremy, I know this is crazy, but would you cut school and drive me tomorrow?"

"Uh . . . no."

"Why not?"

"Crowbar. Remember?"

That stung, despite how much sense it made.

The silence on the line stretched out, broken up by short bursts of static. Siara was about to apologize one more time and hang up when she heard Jeremy sigh.

"Fine. I'll take you," Jeremy said.

Her eyes went wide. "Jeremy, thank you so, so much . . . I don't know how—"

"Oh, wait. I can't. I've got to do something with my parents tomorrow morning. The next day. I'll take you the morning after the demo. It'll give everyone a chance to calm down anyway."

"But—"

"Come on, Siara, that's the best you're going to get out of me. And no crowbars."

"Okay. Thanks. Sorry."

"Yeah. I'll talk to you soon."

She heard the vague electronic click that told her Jeremy had ended the call. She couldn't believe how pushy she was being.

"Siara?" her mother called from the hallway. "Are you ready? I don't want to be late, honey."

After the demo. After tomorrow night. Funny how Jeremy echoed her father, as if he'd somehow listened in. She felt a draft against her back, then turned to see her window, still half-open, still waiting. She put her hands back on the white wooden frame, deciding. Her fingers felt cold from the outdoor air. Winter was coming.

She pushed the window shut.

"I'm ready, Mom."

There had to be *some* way to live in two worlds, at least for a little while.

4. As if it were a small football, Jeremy Gronson tossed the cell phone toward his bed. It spun on its axis, followed a straight line, hit the thick quilt, and neatly buried itself in the folds.

Touchdown.

It had worked. When he dialed Siara's number on one cell, his second phone also rang. All he had to do was manipulate the life trail of Albert Mendt, a phone repairman working on the line. Jeremy fixed things so that Albert was so busy thinking about having enough money to send his son to college, he "accidentally" crossed a few of the wires he was working on. Then Jeremy had a wrench tumble out of the phone man's pocket, distracting poor Albert yet again, so that he sealed up his work without double-checking it.

Now Jeremy could monitor Siara's calls in case someone unfortunate like Keller tried to get in touch. And of course Jeremy had graciously agreed to take her to Harry *after* the demo. By then, she, her parents, and two thirds of RAW High School would be dead.

Dead, dead, dead.

As if they ever really existed in the first place.

Having carefully delivered the tea to his appropriately thankful parents some time ago, a more cheerful Jeremy padded back down the thick-carpeted stairs onto the kitchen's cold marble floor to retrieve his own. The rainbow cup, made by his mother during her ceramics phase, felt hot in his fingertips as he lifted it from the coriander blue counter.

He thought about how she was like Siara in a way, always doing that strange art stuff, playing with images, as if that would ever get anyone anywhere. Still, the cup was pretty, like Siara's poem about Sisyphus as a clock. And even that, strangely enough, had turned out to be useful.

He brought the cup to his lips. It was quite a special brew. Each cup gave him about a day's worth of effect. As far as the labs he'd hired were able to determine, some ingredients bore a chemical resemblance to Ketamine, but were much weaker, and in combination with other elements. Jeremy once hoped he'd be able to synthesize the herbs, but Nostradamus and the Obscure Masters were too clever for that. He'd been given just enough to accomplish his initiation task.

How many doses were left in the bag? Ten? Should be plenty.

Carried by the steam, a bitter almond smell rose to

his nose. Impatient, he took a sip and scalded his tongue. His body shivered, but Jeremy refused to give in to the pain. It was, after all, all about control. Whoever kept it the longest got the most toys.

Cup in hand, he headed back upstairs. Before returning to his own room, he checked in on his parents. They lay in a beautiful king-size Tempur-Pedic bed that conformed to the exact shape of their bodies. They were right next to each other, covered by satin sheets, heads and hair resting on satin pillowcases. Their teacups lay atop a neatly folded *New York Times* on Father's bed table. Jeremy pictured Father placing them there carefully, the way he did everything, arranging things perfectly before taking what he thought would just be a little nap.

The long fingers of Mother's artist's hands were above the sheet, intertwined peacefully above her navel. Father's skin was placid. The worry wrinkles in his face had all but disappeared. They seemed much younger, too, both perfectly peaceful, perfectly perfect.

And dead.

Dead, dead, dead.

As if they had ever existed to begin with.

Jeremy took another sip. A slight dizziness washed his senses, numbing him to the liquid's heat. As he returned to his room, he gulped the rest and placed the empty cup on the chessboard and sat in front of the huge picture window with its grand city view.

When he next inhaled, he also felt himself exhale. And though he worked to slow his breathing, he couldn't be sure if it was the breath he was taking that slowed, the one he'd just taken, or the one he was about to take.

This also was an effect of the tea. A special tea, centuries old.

He didn't think he'd been lucky to find it, only that it was the end of a logical sequence of events, the result of all his hard work, his achievements, his hours of study and exercise.

Of course to the *un*initiated, it all would've looked like an accident, especially the way he opened his locker on the first day of junior year and just found the old library book of prophecies by Nostradamus lying there as if left by a careless student. At the time, even he thought it was an accident. He was going to return it to the school library, try to earn some points with the staff, but something about it intrigued him, and he found himself poring over the age-yellowed pages.

At the time, Jeremy Gronson didn't believe for a second that those silly little poems predicted the future, but his parents had insisted he do an extra-credit assignment for probabilities and statistics class, and the book had given him an idea. Nostradamus was famous, world-famous. If Jeremy could understand how his poems worked, why they appealed to so many people, he figured he could design a computer program to generate equally appealing predictions.

That would net him an A-plus for sure. And just in case his program really did wind up predicting the future, he could use it to invest in the stock market and achieve financial freedom from his parents by the time he graduated.

At the time, he thought that last part was just a fantasy. Nevertheless, he studied the Nostradamus quatrains the way he studied everything else, the way his late tutor, Mr. Chabbers, had made him study: completely, thoroughly, doggedly. He looked not so much at the words, but searched for similarities, patterns, a formula.

Months later, he found one, but not at all the sort he expected. The predictions actually contained a code, based on equidistant letter sequences. If you took all of Nostradamus's quatrains, ordered in the way he had numbered them, and used an algorithm to select particular letters, a new poem appeared, along with some numbers. Roughly translated, it read;

Where time is a snake with no head or tail

There dwell among the beasts of fate

Obscure masters of all God's arts

Who practice the highest truths and by confusion reign

Jeremy was thrilled that he found this amazing dance of math and word. He was even more excited by what the message said. Obscure Masters. The title tickled him, especially the "master" part. "All God's arts" was clearly just a superstitious way of saying *everything*. "The highest truths" sounded coolest of all. It seemed so total, so complete.

But he wasn't finished. Not yet. There were still the numbers to figure out. Most of them gave up their secrets easily enough. They formed a longitude and latitude, a location on the globe, centering on Saint-Rémy-de-Provence, France, Nostradamus's birthplace. But there were still two numbers left, an eight and a ten. They puzzled Jeremy for months, that eight and that ten, because his was a mind that had been trained, at all costs, not to ever let go.

The more he obsessed, the more he became convinced he was onto something big, something that might even make up for the fact that he still wasn't the greatest chess player in the world, and instead ranked—"only," as his parents said—sixteenth. He wondered if he'd found a hidden way to the top. A secret, grand success. Book, poem, and numbers burned inside him for months. The school year nearly ended, and he'd never even started his computer program.

Then, by what smaller minds would again see only as some bizarre coincidence, Jeremy heard that his overreaching French teacher was sponsoring a summer trip to France, and one of the stops was Saint-Rémy-de-Provence. That was all it took to convince him. The coincidence was too glaring. The hand of these Obscure

Masters must be behind it. It was then he first suspected they were, in fact, guiding him to them.

He put up with the long wait, with the tour of Paris, with the French girls who he should have been delighted with, until finally they reached Nostradamus's home. When the group came to the exact room the coordinates indicated, he lingered behind until the fat guide, the enthusiastic teacher, and the rest of the students went ahead and left him alone with his dream.

It was only then, in that moment, staring at the cut stones that comprised the walls, that he figured out the final puzzle piece. He counted the stones on the top row from the northeastern corner, eight up, ten to the left.

Giddy as a child on Christmas morning, he tugged at the tenth stone. The oblong stone slipped out easily, as if oiled on all sides. It thudded at his feet and fell prostrate, as if worshipping him. The filthy little bag that had been wedged behind it tumbled into his long-fingered hands as flecks of centuries-old mortar hovered in the air like stars.

He knew then he'd won something better than all the trophies, better than all the girls, better than the rush he got from slamming the pigskin on the grass after making a touchdown and pretending he was hitting Father's or Mother's face with it.

Translating the handwritten note inside the bag alone should have gotten him the A-plus, but he never showed that work to Mrs. Larousa. Instead he followed the directions that told him to keep it a secret and described how to brew the herbs.

Now all that, like the phone repairman's work on Siara's cell, *seemed* an accident. But Jeremy now knew for a fact that the universe was too ordered for that. It had to make sense. It just had to. There were no accidents, just the machinations of Obscure Masters who by confusion reign. And Jeremy, Jeremy was meant to win every game he played, meant to find that small bag, to find the Masters. Meant to triumph.

Anything else would be like a sin.

As his head swam, he saw the sky outside his window darken, lighten, then darken again. Below, the little lives of little people rolled back to insignificant births and ahead to petty deaths. The buildings—the stores, theaters, skyscrapers, the hundred-year-old churches—all rose and fell like ocean waves. Soon all he could distinguish from the blur were the stars in the circling sky as they winked in and out of existence across a billion years, as if they were flecks of mortar floating in the air of Saint-Rémy-de-Provence.

Remembering Siara Warner's fondness for poems, he thought:

I am such stuff as dreams are made on.

With a roar, the world exploded, until everything remained—*the* everything; the endless shifting trails his crushed rival dubbed A-Time, reality raveled into patterns and paths. To the uninitiated, even to Jeremy, it still mostly looked like a big, unruly mess, but the Obscure Masters could see the needles in the haystack, the method in the mess, and they would teach him if he won.

Steadfast, the Initiate strode along the curved surfaces, moving with speed and confidence. In short order he found what he was looking for: Harry Keller's rumbling, bumbling life trail, which vexed him like an unscratchable spider bite.

His nostrils flared as he scanned its surface. Even being near Keller's trail pissed him off. But he had to be sure, so he looked, and looked carefully. Good. There'd been no change. All was as he'd left it after the fire. Keller was hopelessly insane.

He'd come close to getting rid of him before, but now the sedatives and antipsychotics in Keller's bloodstream were preventing him from even entering A-Time, so there was no way for his fate to change again.

Weird how some chemicals could get you there and others keep you out. Weirder still how someone like Keller could get into A-Time without any herbs, but Jeremy needed his tea.

Oh well, the Masters would explain that, too. Jeremy only wished he could have killed Keller. He'd wanted so badly to have Keller die in the fire, but there were too many factors, too many variables. Maybe the fact that Keller was a time walker himself somehow protected him. The closest he could manage was insanity, and for that, Jeremy had had to endure a whack in the skull with a crowbar.

Well, maybe after tomorrow night, he'd try again.

An unexpected rumble caught his attention. Ripples appeared in the trails near Keller's future. They shifted in unison, like choreographed serpents, making room for a new arrival.

This again?

Jeremy grimaced. He was annoyed, but only slightly surprised, to see Siara's trail veering back toward Harry's in the near future.

Tweedledum on her way to save Tweedledee.

It looked like she might try to arrive at Windfree tomorrow afternoon.

Had she found another ride? Was she planning to hitch? This was such a pain in the ass. No matter how many times, no matter how many ways Jeremy tried to separate them, they came together. He'd even dated her himself, just to keep them apart, but they kept growing toward one another, like weeds. It was another puzzle. How could Siara reject him, over and over, against all common sense, for that addled sack of crap? He once thought she'd seemed so smart, but she was obviously a loser, too.

If Keller ever did die, her trail would probably spend the rest of its time circling the point where he died, forever, like the clock in her stupid poem.

But Jeremy had other plans for her, and now he had to seal the deal.

Fighting a feeling of disgust, he drove his strong, long-fingered hands deep into the muck of Harry and felt his way around, turning his head to the side, as if it smelled like a cesspool.

His sense of revulsion was worse than the scalding tea, almost worse than killing his parents. But it was all about control. Concentrating, he shaped this part, pulled at that. He was tickled to think he was getting better at it, or maybe he just wasn't having as much interference. Now that Keller was stuck in linear time, his life was just like anyone else's.

Just like anyone else's.

Hmm. Maybe he *could* kill him.

Soon, the desired changes rattled through Keller's already-dismal future, shortening it considerably. His fingers still in the trail, Jeremy saw Keller's end quite clearly:

"Please!" the white-haired cop said. "Don't do it. The negotiator will be here in just a second and she'll know just what to say. Just wait a little while . . . please!"

No! We've waited so long! Just jump!

Tough choice. Who to believe?

Harry looked out at the world, at the tops of the buildings, the little people down below, connected by so many things, disconnected by so few. Subject to disease and war, one hand reaching for the stars, the other slinking back to the darkest cave. And all this time, he thought it somehow all made sense, that he could figure it out.

But he was wrong.

"When you're right, you're right," he said to himself, to the Fool. "It doesn't make any sense. Not one bit."

He turned to look at the cop. "I'm really sorry about this, he said.

The cop lunged forward to grab him, but Harry smiled, shrugged, and let the Quirk-shard move his feet over the ledge.

Briefly, Harry felt weightless, just like he had so many years ago, trapped in his father's arms at the top of an amusement park ride. There'd be no parachute this time, though. His stomach lurched. Everything spun. He was expecting to fly, but the Fool had lied. He wasn't flying. He was falling. It would all be over in seconds.

Thanks, so so much! the Quirk-shard said.

"Don't mention it," Harry answered, falling faster and faster.

Grinning wickedly, Jeremy pulled his hands from the muck. He wondered why Keller never figured out that you didn't have to be *in* a trail to *see* what was in it. Probably because he was an idiot. That was why he'd die this time for sure. That was why Jeremy would win.

Nearby, Jeremy's Quirk yipped merrily at the changes. It extended its single eye beyond the row of teeth that formed its mouth, to ferret out a spot for itself in Keller.

When it did, and as it stuffed its eye deep into the delicious cranny, Siara's life—like a large blind worm—veered away, back toward the fate Jeremy planned for it. When it reached his massive sculpture, his master-piece, Siara's life trail was sucked in like a piece of spaghetti into the mouth of a starving demon.

It was locked now, as if with a key. A keystone.

It was done. Really done.

Now there's nothing that can save either of you. Nothing.

5. *Nothing. Zero. The Fool.*

The giant loomed above Harry Keller, the size of a Thanksgiving Day balloon. No, bigger. Much bigger. It was the size of the whole damn Thanksgiving Day parade. Its moon-size eyes twinkled. The wide swath of red that circled its cheeks elongated its mad smile so it covered half the huge white face.

As Harry lay on his back, cowering, an image popped into his mind; a card from Aunt Shirley's tarot deck, the one with the vagabond staring at the sky as he merrily marched off a cliff, a small dog nipping at his heels. The image didn't comfort him, it only frightened him more. Panicked questions rushed from his mouth like rats deserting a sinking ship: "Who? What? Where?"

"YES! YES AND YES!" the clown boomed back.

Harry raised his arms to protect himself, not from the big clown, but from the words. Each YES set Harry's body bouncing and sent a swarm of sights, sounds, and feelings careening through his head; smiley faces, a parent handing him sticky candy, a girl's moist kiss, an A-plus scribbled in blue pen on a paper, Siara visiting his apartment. Every possible derivation, manifestation, and connotation of YES hit him like a fist, as if the meaning-volume of his soul's ears had been turned up full.

Harry thought he was being killed, but when the inner onslaught ended, miraculously, he wasn't only still alive, he was thinking clearer, cleaner, as if the giant's words had burned some of his madness away.

Harry looked around. Glimpses of life trails, Quirks, Glitches, and drifting Timeflys poked from between the enormous polka-dot folds of the clown's floppy pant-legs. He was in A-Time. Despite the drugs, he'd gone timeless.

How?

"Because I brought you here," the clown responded, though Harry's question hadn't been asked out loud.

Its lips parted into a grin, revealing again its massive white teeth and horrid pink tongue. It looked awful happy. Was that a good thing? Better than having it angry, Harry supposed.

"Are you going to kill me?" It seemed as good a time as any to ask.

It shook its head. "We're not enemies, Harry. This isn't *Godzilla versus Cremora*."

"Umm . . . isn't that Gammera?"

"No. Cremora. Seems the big lizard is lactose intolerant."

When Harry didn't react, the clown's face turned serious.

"It's a joke. Get it?"

Harry just stared at it. *Yeah, a* bad *joke . . .*

"No, a good one." It opened its cavernous mouth and laughed, releasing a gale that pushed Harry's body deep into the terrain beneath him.

The clown raised an eyebrow. "See? A joke. You should lighten up a little, y'know?"

Harry raised himself from the Harry-shaped hole that had formed beneath him. "Lighten up? How can I, with you haunting me, ever since . . . ever since . . ."

"Yes?" the clown asked.

Ever since what?

Harry realized he'd been seeing the clown since his father died. Ever since he was struck by lightning when the preacher asked God to do just that. Like a joke. Like a big, bad joke, a killer punch line no joker could resist.

Like Godzilla versus Cremora.

Emotion overwhelmed Harry's fear. "Did you kill my father?"

The giant's head shook gently from side to side. "Not exactly. Closer to say I *am* your father's death."

Harry's body shivered, but his brow furrowed defiantly. "What's that supposed to mean?"

The clown gave him a half smile. "That I manifest in certain events. I'm an archetype, Harry, the visible face of a god. Specifically, the Fool, the Trickster, Azeban, Brer Rabbit, Aunt Nancy, Bamapana, Tezcatlipoca, Puck, the Monkey King, Satan, Renart the Fox, Bugs Bunny, Prometheus, Hermes Trismegistus, Coyote, Kokopelli, Kantjil, Amaguq, Kitsune, Mantis, Nasreddin, Loki, Sosruko, Nanabush, Maui, Agu Tonpa, Cin-an-ev, Baron Samedi, Anansi, Eshu, Ozat, Meribank, even Spongebob Squarepants . . ."

Just like the YESes that came before, each name carried a score of impressions: steamy African veldts, windswept North American plains, smoky European cities, places of heat, of cold, and all the temperatures in between.

Harry shook his head, trying to shed the maelstrom, and said, "You're the balloon. The one that led me to Todd and Melody."

"Yes."

"I thought you were a memory, a statue at Dreamland. Just something left over from childhood."

"That, too. Just not *just*."

An archetype. A god. Sure. According to Jung and Campbell, they were the building blocks of the human mind. Of course, you weren't supposed to be able to chat with them. But if it were true, Harry was staring at something created by the timeless energies of everyone on the planet, past, present, and future. Everyone.

Maybe it *was* a god.

A glint appeared in the Fool's eyes. From its expression, Harry could tell it'd heard each of his thoughts and found his despair amusing.

Harry swallowed. "Am I imagining you, like I did Elijah?"

The clown chuckled. "Yes and no. You have to be able to imagine to see me, but it's really more like redistricting—same pie, different slices."

"Redistricting? Redistricting what? What kind of pie?"

Its huge index finger poked Harry in the chest. He felt as if he were being tapped with the base of a telephone pole. "The self-pie. Like Elijah said, it has loose boundaries. Slice it one way and you might find your feminine side, like Elijah, but slice it deep enough and you wind up outside again, where you'll find something like me."

A giant white glove reached down and squeezed Harry's hopelessly tiny hand between its massive thumb and finger. It took him a moment to realize the thing was shaking hands with him.

"Congratulations. You the man. You made it all the way to nothing."

"Uh . . . thanks?"

It pulled, yanking Harry into a seated position. Then it crossed its legs and sat in front of him.

"You're welcome, but let's get down to it. You've got questions, I've got answers, some of which may even be true. Before we go any further, I want to spell out the deal. You ask whatever you like, and I'll answer, but for every question you ask, I'm going to hit you, really, really hard."

Without thinking, Harry asked, "Why would you do that?"

SWAT!

The next thing Harry knew, he was skidding along the terrain, scraping the uneven surfaces like a rock skimming ripples in a pond. When he finally slowed, rolled, and settled into a moaning heap, the giant Fool trotted up, shaking the trails with his steps—*thud, thud, thud.*

It leaned over and looked at the fallen Harry. "Because I feel like it."

Harry touched the side if his face. No bruises. He felt his arm and ribcage. No broken bones. Everything hurt though. Still, he couldn't keep from asking, "Can you tell me how to stop Jeremy, save Siara, and get rid of the Quirk inside me?"

WHACK!

Again, Harry flew, crashed, rolled, slowed, and stopped. Again, the Fool trotted up—*thud, thud, thud*

"That was three questions, but since there's one answer, I'll let it go. No. You have to figure that out yourself. I'm not your advisor. I'm more like the scorpion in the fable. You know, he can't get across the river so he asks the frog for a ride? The frog says, Are you nuts? You'll sting me! The scorpion says, Why would I sting you? I'd drown, too. So the frog says okay. Halfway across, the scorpion stings him. The dying frog asks, What'd you do that for? The drowning scorpion says, Sorry, it's my nature.

"Me, I'm a force for chaos and I don't act out of character. In fact, I'm not even really helping you. I just am. You move closer or farther away from me."

But why? Harry thought, just barely managing to keep from asking out loud. Again, the expression on the thing's face told Harry it knew what he was thinking. It was waiting, smiling, probably looking forward to thwacking him again.

Biding his time, Harry rubbed his jaw.

Bemused, the Fool said, "You know, you don't *have* to ask me anything if you don't want to. But this is where we're alike, see? You're like the scorpion, too. You're going to ask, even though you know you'll get thwacked. Then I'll hit you and you'll get up and ask again. That's what I like about you, Harry."

It was right. Despite the certain pain, questions raced each other to his mouth.

"What's the voice I hear when I look in someone's trail?"

THUNK!

Thud, thud, thud

"Your filter, talking back. It does what's easiest—turns everything into a story."

"Why could Todd Penderwhistle enter his life trail when I can't enter mine?"

SHUNK!

This time after he hit the ground, Harry rolled for what felt like a half mile, slamming his side and shoulders into the curved tops of trail after trail before he finally came to a stop.

But the Fool knew where to find him. *Thud, thud, thud.*

"That you probably could have figured out yourself. Ever see anyone *other* than you unable to enter their own past?"

"Uh . . . no."

"That's because the rules of your filter don't permit *you* to enter your life trail. It's the way you set things up."

Harry shook his head. "That doesn't make sense. It's a rule of A-Time. I didn't make this place up—the Quirks, the Glitches, the trails! I just named them! I only see it because my linear-time filter *isn't* working. I don't control reality!" Harry said.

"No," the Fool answered. "You don't. But you create and control yourself. Scorpion stings the turtle. Harry gets answers in a way that thwacks him. Language makes the world. It's better to hear your name than to see your face. Get it? It's a joke. *Godzilla versus Cremora.* And you really should lighten up a little."

"But . . . ," Harry began. He gritted his teeth, trying to come up with the right phrasing. He thought he had it once or twice, but he didn't want to get hit for nothing.

As it waited, the Fool lay down in front of him, flopping on its belly across the terrain, resting its head on its white-gloved hands. It raised its gargantuan feet up, crossing them at the ankles and letting the moon-sized bells on its boots jingle. They sounded like the chimes of a thousand churches.

Its eyes glistened. It smiled invitingly.

"Go ahead," it whispered. "Ask. You know you want to; you want to bad. And yeah, I know the answer."

The words appeared on the tip of Harry's tongue, as if the Fool had conjured them. It was the question Harry's father had always wanted him to answer. So he asked:

"How *does* reality work?"

It used a full fist on him this time, and didn't hold back.

POW!

There was pain, great pain, really, really great pain, then flying, falling, landing—*thud, thud, thud*—and an answer at last.

"It doesn't," the Fool said.

Harry's head listed to the side. He worried he might pass out, but he didn't. It was a cheap answer. A cheat. The world had to make sense—it just had to.

The Fool shook its head. "Working, not working,

they're *all* just what you call filters. They're masks really. Everything is. Everything. Got that? *Everything*. All that terrifying, life-taking, debilitating, crippling, killing, overpowering, numbing, cracking, crunching, hating, separating, cultivating, inspiring, integrating, degradating, carbon-dating, creating, writhing, withering, deadening, deciding, hoping, coping, loping, doping, troping, trapping, winking, thinking, tree-hugging, exonerating, ozone-depleting, freedom-fighting, resource-wasting, conservating, renovating, aggravating, abdicating, syncopating, calculating, blinking, blanking, indicating, medicating, habituating, levitating, eradicating, irritating, flagellating, focusing, locusing, heat-seeking, exiting, activating, scintillating, decapitating, transposing, excruciating, invigorating, pixelating, cherry-picking, gerrymandering, deficit-spending, crawling, falling, mauling, calling, scrawling, scrolling, rolling, doling, molting, gloating, kicking, mixing, fixing, nixing, abstaining, abstracting, faxing, adultering, appropriating, backtracking, bloodsucking, counterpunching, nesting, resting, besting, testing, cresting, jesting, knowing, glowing, fascinating, compromising, condescending, fixating, obfuscating, breathtaking, whitening, brightening, canceling, carousing, normalizing, corroborating, agitating, characterizing, epitomizing, fantasizing, cleansing, clouting, clowning, lightly browning, napkin-tying, flirting, blurting, burning, boring, whirring, turning, tracing, facing, lacing, devastating, ingratiating, energizing, finalizing stuff is a mask, just a mask. And me, I'm one of them. And what you think of as yourself is another."

As before, each word flooded his mind with a million pictures, feelings, and smells, but this time there was no release. They kept coming, stacked miles high, words upon words, worlds upon worlds, lining up to invade his skull, as if he were chained to a rock as Niagara Falls came down upon him forever. And every single thought, even the smallest, felt as if it were being written in white fire in the darkest depths of his brain.

And when it was finally, impossibly over, nothing lingered. It just raced through him without leaving a trace.

Confused, staggered, exhausted, Harry Keller managed to say, "So . . . nothing's real?"

A big open-handed white-gloved hand swept toward him, slapping him full-body.

WHUNK! Thud, thud, thud.

"Of course it is! Masks are real!"

"So . . . nothing's important?"

Again the hand rushed him, knocking him back a hundred yards. The terrain he landed in this time—dark, shapeless, and cold—was utterly unfamiliar, Harry wasn't sure if it was past or future or if he was even still in A-Time at all. The only recognizable thing was the most horrific—the grinning giant that stormed up to him.

Thud, thud, thud.

"Of course it is! Masks are incredibly important. Ralph Waldo Emerson said all we ever deal with are surfaces, and what's a surface if not a mask?"

"So . . . if it's real and important, what's the difference if it's all a mask or not?"

Harry winced and closed his eyes, bracing himself for the blow. When it didn't come, he slowly peeked out above his raised arm.

That was when the Fool slapped him again.

PHWAT!

He burst through a flock—an hour?—of Timeflys, and landed in a section of A-Time colored completely in shades of blue.

"Tsk, tsk!" the Fool boomed as it thudded up. "The point, Harry, is that even if everything you see is a mask, there still must be something *beneath* it. Masks may be the only way you have to understand things, but they're not where everything lives."

It smiled. Harry furrowed his brow.

"Where *do* we live?"

He winced, buried his head in his shoulders, but this time the blow never came. Instead the Fool bent down, parted his enormous lips and whispered, gentle as a summer breeze, "Under the mask. You know, you can see when you're wrong, but you can't always see when you're right. You were right about a lot, all on your own. Filters shape the way people see the world. But you didn't free yourself from them; you just built a new one. A-Time is just another filter, still not the last word. Not a higher reality, not a lower one, just a different mask from what you were used to. Here, watch."

The giant snapped its fingers and the hard past became soft, the soft future hard. Another snap returned things to normal: hard past, soft future.

If normal was ever what it was.

But the clown wasn't done. It waved its hand across the terrain. The Event Horizon, the sizzling line that stretched from one end of A-Time to another, the line that always moved, writing future into past, stopped short and moved back and forth a few times, like a windshield wiper.

Harry shook. He'd discovered this new world when his old one fell apart, thought it was bigger, sturdier, but here it was collapsing, too. You just couldn't find a good reliable reality these days.

And the Fool wasn't done yet. It pinched Harry's face between its fingers and came close.

"Pay attention. Here's the prize. The only time you're ever even *close* to reality is when you've just chucked one mask and haven't had a chance yet to pick up another. It only lasts a moment, but moments can last forever. When you really want things to change, find that moment."

Harry shook his head. He furrowed his brow. He scrunched up his face.

"That doesn't make any sense." *And it all has to make sense! It has to!*

The Fool shook its head. "Thinking the world *has* to make sense is like using a screwdriver on a nail. Wrong tool. The world has sense *in* it, but it's bigger than sense. It's the Atman, you know, like Batman without the *B*? The All."

"Like Ball without a B?"

WHAP!

Harry went flying. But this time, a giant hand caught him, and he found himself staring into the Fool's enormous pupils, two swarming blacknesses that looked like the primordial seas in which life formed, the waters above which God's spirit hovered in the moments before creation. And in that dark, the clown's voice boomed:

"Exactly! Saying everything is an illusion is as meaningless as saying everything's real. All things are contained in the world—good, bad, day, night, sense, nonsense—so everything *has* to be more than just sense. Make sense?"

Harry scrunched his face. "Is that a trick question?"

WHAM!

Rather than flying through the air, Harry felt his torso crunch into his legs as the force of the blow drove him not up, but deep into the terrain. When he opened his eyes, he saw he was pinned, buried up to his neck. The Fool, Harry realized, had made a fist, and used it to drive Harry into the ground.

Smiling all the while, the clown of his childhood, the clown of his visions, the clown of his nightmares, reached out and ripped Harry's head off.

It was funny seeing his own headless body like that, funnier still as the Fool seemed to warp and suck itself into the base of Harry's neck, pulling itself bit by bit into his aching skull. Harry's head was so full of Fool he thought it would pop. Instead, his head just floated gently down, back onto his neck where, he supposed, it belonged.

Though the Fool was inside him now, he could still see it winking, still hear it whisper, as it said, "They're *all* trick questions."

6. Harry opened his eyes. He was back in his padded cell. Blinking, he felt the familiar sleepy grit around his eyes. The ceiling was right where it had been, no sign it'd been torn off by the hands of a god.

What about the book? Wasn't there a book?

It was gone, too.

The extreme clarity he'd enjoyed in the presence of the Fool had also vanished. Aside from the eye-jam, he was groggy, dry-mouthed, again feeling the numbing drugs course through his veins, making his every thought march through a bog.

It was likely he'd imagined it. After all, even in his addled memory, talking to the Fool felt a lot like talking to himself. Only worse.

A-Time was real, though; he knew that. The things he saw there affected linear time, changed destinies, saved or ended lives. Unless he'd been imagining every-thing.

And saying everything's fake is the same as saying everything's real, isn't it?

And no matter where you go, there you are.

Was there anything, anything at all different in the cell? Anything that could prove something had actually happened somewhere other than in his head? He strained his neck left, then right, looked around, scanned every inch of whiteness, hoping for anything that might be even slightly out of place.

White walls, floor, ceiling. And, well, there was the door. That was different.

It was open.

Open?

Light from the hallway was flooding in, highlighting the stains on the canvas.

Can it be? Can I get out?

Excited, he tried to stand, but his legs were too wobbly. He flopped to his side, unable to stop his fall because his arms were pinned by the straitjacket.

Ungh!

Since he was lying down now, the drugs wanted him to fall asleep, but he couldn't miss this opportunity, not with the door just open like that. He rolled onto his back, then used his legs to push himself along the floor until he hit the wall. He bent his head forward and kept pushing, flattening his torso. Slowly, he wriggled his back up the coarse surface, and once he was up high enough, he stood.

Feeling like a drugged, giant white penguin, Harry waddled across the springy surface to the open door. Cautiously, he peered into the hall. It was thin and severe, a gray flatness interrupted only by several thick doors—more cells, containing fellow crazy people. Every other ceiling light was off. That meant it was late. They conserved power at night, left on only what they needed.

But the most interesting thing in his field of vision was Jesus, the guard. He was lying in a heap in the center of the floor, snoring.

"Wow," Harry said, surprised.

At the sound of Harry's voice, Jesus snorfled and smacked his lips.

Crap! Harry thought, wishing he could slap his pinned hands over his stupid mouth.

Jesus moaned slightly, twitched, then snored again.

Lighten up, hell. What I really need to learn to do is keep my stupid mouth shut!

Satisfied the guard was out, he tiptoed over quietly and saw two bottles on the floor near the sleeping body, one of ibuprofen, the other sleeping pills, their contents spilled. The little white pills looked remarkably alike. An image flashed in Harry's head of Jesus, his head throbbing, mixing up his pills and suffering the consequences.

Quite the coincidence. Like the door. Exactly the sort of thing Harry would expect from someone mucking around in A-Time. Maybe the Fool, the big lug, was helping him escape. Whatever. No reason to look a gift horse in the mouth.

The linoleum in the hallway was cold compared to the padding, and his feet were only protected by the thin cloth coverings that passed for a crazy person's shoes. He padded quickly to the end of the hall, only to find the door to the stairwell locked. A card reader was mounted on the wall next to the silver door-handle.

Damn.

He waddled back to the guard. It didn't look like there was anything in his shirt, but he saw the tip of an old brown wallet jutting from the pants pocket, the fabric stretched thin by Jesus's enormous butt.

Carefully, gently, Harry went down to his knees, put his face near the butt, and used his teeth to pull at the wallet.

Please don't let anyone see me like this. . . .

With a bit of tugging, it slid free and landed on the floor. Harry kicked it away from Jesus, then, using his nose, managed to unfold it and pull sundry plastic cards free—credit card, license, library card, and yeah, Windfree employee ID.

Getting the thin, flat plastic rectangle up from the floor proved the hardest part. Harry nearly broke a tooth trying to pry the card up but finally managed it. Card in teeth, he waddled back to the door, slid the card through the reader, and pressed the handle.

Click.

Now he was in the stairwell, leaning against the door with his shoulder, looking down at the concrete and steel stairs that led to the floors below.

Ha! I made it! Now it's down to the basement, and maybe I can sneak out of the building! Or better yet, up, up, up to the roof where I can jump off! The building must be six, seven flights. That should be high enough to—

Wait a minute! What am I thinking?

But it wasn't him thinking at all. It was the Quirkshard. With the sedatives and antipsychotics in him, Harry's will was weak, and the shard had no such vulnerabilities. His body wavered at the top of the stairs. He wanted to walk down, but the shard was pulling him in the opposite direction.

Down, boy! Down!

No! Up, up, up!

Much to his chagrin, Harry watched his right foot move onto the stairway headed up, followed by his left. He pulled back, but not too hard, so it wasn't a very effective pull. Being in a straitjacket, he didn't want to pull hard enough to make himself fall. In a few seconds, despite his efforts, he was halfway up the stairs.

Not good. Definitely not good.

Step, step, step.

He could shout for help, if the shard let him, but then he'd just be tossed back in his cell.

Step, step, step.

Maybe there was something he could do in A-Time. He concentrated, trying to conjure the timeless state. The edges of the stairwell lights got a little blurry, but it was no use. The drugs were keeping him in linear time.

How had the Fool gotten him into A-Time? Maybe because he was a god and gods could pretty much do whatever the hell they wanted. Or maybe, if Harry could infest other people with his thoughts, giving them temporary access to A-Time, the Fool had just done the same to Harry.

What had the Fool said about finding a new mask?

Step, step, step.

He reached the first landing and rounded it.

Heh. The thought was so strange. An archetype generating a state of mind in Harry. Weren't archetypes just made up of people? Lots of people, yes . . . unless maybe it was the other way around, and people were made up of archetypes.

Weird.

Step, step, step.

There were more pressing issues at hand. The next flight was coming up. The Quirk was practically singing:

Jump, Harry! Jump! Jump, jump. jump!

At the next landing, he bit his tongue, hard. Pain lit his nervous system. His body reflexively jumped backward, into a wall. For a scant few seconds, the jumping urge disappeared. Harry used the moments to veer toward the door. He opened it, stepped into another hall, and slammed it shut.

No, no, no! Jump, jump, jump!

He pushed his back into the door, but his feet already wanted to resume the climb. Maybe he could lock himself in a closet and wait for the drugs to wear off so he could fight the Quirk-shard.

What was around him here? Again, half the lights were off. That was good news. The night staff at Windfree was less than half that of the day shift. Still, they checked on him at least every hour, and Jesus wouldn't stay asleep forever. It was only a matter of time before they realized he was gone. With a patient loose, the building would go into lockdown and he'd be trapped again.

But how could he escape if he couldn't trust his own damn feet?

He panted, and noticed he was only a few yards from another godsend: a wall phone. If he couldn't escape, at least he could warn Siara about her "boyfriend," who was secretly the master of all evil in the world.

Harry walked over and nudged the receiver off the cradle with his forehead. It sailed down the length of its cord, then bounced in the air like a bungee jumper. The dial tone was clearly audible. Using his nose, he punched a nine to get an outside line, then dialed Siara's number.

It rang once, twice, and a familiar voice answered the phone.

"Keller?" it said, quite startled. "Harry Keller?"

"Jeremy Gronson?" Harry answered back, equally surprised.

There was a silence for a few moments, then, "Keller, why aren't you dead?"

Hearing that, Harry knew in a flash it was true, all true. Jeremy Gronson was the Daemon, the one who'd been stalking him in A-Time, the one who'd controlled Melody, who'd controlled Todd. *The one who was dating Siara.*

Harry gritted his teeth and hissed, "You just did me the biggest favor in the world, you bastard. You just proved I'm not insane."

"No, Keller," Jeremy answered. "The biggest favor would be to put you out of your misery and kill you. But don't worry, I'll get to it. And by the way? You *are* insane. Totally."

With a click the line went dead. Harry knew what would happen next. Gronson would go to A-Time and rearrange his trail so he'd wind up back in the cell, or worse.

Adrenaline surged through his body. When he thought of the danger Siara was in, the suicide voice yielded with a whimper. He ran full tilt down the center of the hall, looking for an exit. As he did, one by one, all the lights came on.

Jeremy was doing his thing in A-Time. How long did Harry have left? A minute? A second? He kept running. A bulletin board came loose from the wall, nearly tripping him, but Harry jumped over it. Soapy water sloshed across the floor from an unseen bucket, but he stopped and raced the other way.

At a corner he turned. There, down the long institutional hall, fifty yards away, was the red-and-white light of an emergency exit sign.

Footsteps came from behind; voices shouted. A door opened and a thin nurse wearing horn-rimmed glasses stepped out. She looked instantly repulsed when she saw Harry, as if he were some bad food she could swear she'd thrown away. Harry just smiled back.

He dove to her side, nearly fell, but caught himself and picked up speed. He was there, almost there, almost at the exit. He could taste it, could feel the handle give, feel the door open at his push, sense the cold outside air against his face.

He was just about convinced he'd made it when he felt something in his chest that made him stop short. All of a sudden, his body wouldn't respond. Something twisted in his gut, moved his arms this way instead of that. It was a strange sensation, one he'd never experienced before, as if someone had stuck their fingers into him, into his soul, into his future, and was yanking things around.

Jeremy.

Harry twisted, gasped and fell. In no time they were upon him, shouting, calling for a needle. As the sharp tip plunged into his arm, he remembered that the outside of the building was surrounded by a fence. He'd never have made it out anyway.

Tasting anger on his tongue as if it were the bitter tea, the Initiate yanked his hands out of Harry Keller's life and wondered, *How on earth did he get back in play?*

Blowing air through his nostrils, he straightened, feeling his black robes tumble back down around his arms.

"Unk?"

His Quirk looked at him pleadingly, whining, wondering what was going on. It thought it was going to happen, then all of a sudden it didn't. It was tired of being yanked around.

"Unk!"

The Initiate kicked it, slamming it with the heel of his foot. With a pained howl, it ran off and hid behind a small bubbly hill in the future, occasionally sticking its single eye out from beyond the rim to look sheepishly at its master.

The Initiate turned away and closed his eyes to the terrain, to everything, so he could think. His brain strained, trying to hold all the possibilities, wondering what happened. If it wasn't for the phone call tipping Jeremy off, Keller might have done it, might have reached that door and freedom.

But how? He'd checked it over a million times. There was nothing, nothing in Keller's trail that could explain the seeming accidents, no sign his life had been interfered with by anyone other than the Initiate himself, no indication he was anything other than trapped, trapped in Windfree, trapped in linear time. But still he'd almost gotten out.

It would take something just shy of a god to create those sorts of coincidences and not leave so much as a mark behind.

A god, or a Master.

He paused and opened his mouth into a small circle.

So, was it them? Is this another part of my Initiation?

They'd always spoken of Keller as if he was just a distraction from his trial, but maybe that was a trick.

Yes. It made sense. It fit the facts. The Obscure Masters had put that bumbling fool in his way to test his wherewithal. Keller was a straw dog, and they were protecting him. That was why Jeremy couldn't kill him, why he kept resurfacing.

That was it, it had to be. Keller was part of his test.

He whistled to the Quirk. It hesitated, smarting from the kick, so he had to whistle twice more. Cautiously, it trotted out and presented itself. It shied away a bit when the Initiate put out his hand, but it warmed as he patted it.

"Unk! Unk!"

"There, there. Sorry I was angry," Jeremy said. "It's all right now. I think I understand. I just have to change my plans again."

Siara was half-asleep when the phone rang, but she grabbed it immediately, if only to stop the tone from waking her parents. The CID was clear enough even through her sleepy eyes.

"Jeremy? It's after one in the morning."

"I know," he said, sounding apologetic. "I was just feeling bad about how we left things. I know you're worried about Harry, so I figure my parents will keep. They'll be fine where they are for a while. If you still want, I'll drive you to see him tomorrow morning."

"Jeremy, really? I can't believe it! You are so . . . you're . . . you're the best ex-boyfriend, ever! The best!" Siara said.

She didn't know to what great and wonderful stroke of luck she owed this bizarre change, she only knew that tomorrow morning she'd be on her way to see Harry.

7. *Every life is like colored thread in a blanket that has no beginning or end.*

Jeffrey Tippicks's words haunted his son as he maneuvered his old Toyota hatchback past the iron front gate of Windfree Sanitarium. Emeril Tippicks still had his headache from yesterday; the aspirin hadn't helped in the least. Every time he'd hesitated at a light and the car behind him honked, he'd thought the sound would kill him.

At least the air was cleaner this far north of the city, doubly so after last night's rainstorm. The building's quiet browns and whites were soothing, like mountain rock peering from forested hills. It had been built as a private home in the 1920s in a grand palatial style, but thick bars were now crudely bolted over each window, and a vast, gaudy, steel-mesh net hung over the roof.

And this is where my father died.

Head pounding, Tippicks tried to maneuver his small car into a tight space near the entrance. A slight pressure on the wheel and a horrid sound told him he hadn't made it. He pushed at the door, chagrined to find he was too close to the next car for it to open all the way. He struggled, barely able to squeeze out, and saw the long, deep scratch his bumper had made on an otherwise shiny BMW.

Annoyed, he slammed the car door, snagging his tweed jacket in it. Pulling it free, he tore a button off and earned a long smear of black grease above the pocket.

What was wrong with him today?

He thought about leaving a note for the owner but then checked his watch: 9:12 A.M. He'd have to move fast if he wanted to speak to Keller and make it back to school before lunch.

Speak to Keller. And ask him what?

Why do you see what my father saw? Can you tell me if I'm insane myself to be here? Despite the pain, he chuckled, realizing it was the perfect place to go mad, like having your car break down in front of a gas station.

He tried to wipe the grease from his jacket but only succeeded in covering his hands. Still rubbing them, Tippicks tried to maneuver around a thick branch on the sidewalk, knocked down by last night's storm, but only succeeded in stepping in a puddle.

His shoes wet now, he passed between the stone columns at the front entrance, opened the glass and aluminum door, and stepped into the waiting room. It was small, with barely enough space for a couch and a potted plant. There weren't even any magazines. It looked as if no one ever waited here.

A blue-haired woman seated behind a Plexiglas screen was roused from her paperwork at the sound of the opening door. Tippicks stepped up, trying to look cheerful, and immediately knocked over a cupful of pens that sat on the small counter in front of her. He rolled his eyes as they clattered to his feet.

"I have an appointed with Dr. Shinn," he said, bending to pick them up.

She didn't answer, but as Tippicks recovered the last of the pens, a buzzer sounded. A pleasant Asian man stepped out from an inner door and extended his hand.

"Mr. Tippicks. You're here to see Harry Keller."

"Yes," Tippicks said, shaking his hand, forgetting about the grease. Remembering the scratch, he added, "Do you know who owns that green BMW outside?"

Shinn's grin widened. "It's mine. Brand new. Do you like it?"

Tippicks tried to smile. "Oh, yes. Wonderful car."

Dr. Shinn waved Tippicks in and guided him into an elevator. As the numbers above the closed doors indicated they were going up, Tippicks rattled off what he knew about Harry, the trauma, the erratic behavior, but also the sparks of lucidity.

Shinn eyed him with disapproval. "The boy does all this, has all these strange behaviors, but up until he goes totally berserk, you think he's fine?"

Tippicks felt himself turning red as the elevator stopped and the doors creaked open. Nervous, he rubbed the grease on his palm with his thumb. "I just thought he had a chance to recover on his own. That it would be better that way for him."

Shinn shook his head and exited. Silent, he slipped his card through a reader and led Tippicks into a narrow hallway. When they reached the third door, he motioned for Tippicks to look through its small window.

"Here is the young man you thought could recover on his own," he said.

Tippicks leaned in toward the glass and frowned. Curled up in a far corner of the padded room was what looked like a pile of dirty linen. The unruly brown mop of hair on its top was the only thing indicating it was a human being.

Shin shrugged. "He's been violent since he arrived. Lashed out at the ambulance attendants, gave our interns some nasty bruises. Tried to escape last night. We've doubled his meds, so he's pretty calm now. I doubt he can even stand."

Unable to conceal his anger, Tippicks asked, "If you've got him so doped up that he can't move, why is he still in a straitjacket?"

Shinn opened his mouth to explain when the mop of hair rustled. Both men turned as Harry Keller raised his head, brown eyes peering through strands of long, dirty hair.

"Mr. Tippicks?" Harry said hoarsely.

Shinn's annoyance fled. "He's responding to your

voice. He didn't even respond to his aunt. He hasn't spoken to anyone since he's been here."

"Yes, Harry," Tippicks called through the door. "It's me."

Harry struggled to his feet and slouched toward the door. He rested his forehead against the window, giving them a perfect view of his haggard face as his shallow breath made little clouds on the dirty glass.

"Hi, Mr. Tippicks," Harry said.

"Hi, Harry. How are you?" Tippicks said back. Harry was always pale, but now he looked jaundiced. The spark Tippicks had often seen in his eyes was gone, replaced by a dull sheen, like a marble covered in thick grease.

"Been better."

"I can see that. Harry, if I can get Dr. Shinn to take you out of there for a while to talk to me, will you promise to behave, not to run away?"

Harry's brow furrowed. He looked down at his feet.

"You mean, I'm not running?" he said.

"Harry."

He looked up and blinked. "Yeah. Sure. Promise. I'd cross my heart, but . . ."

Tippicks turned to Shinn, whose mouth was still open wide.

"What do you think, Dr. Shinn?" Tippicks asked. "Can you bring him out of there so I can talk to him?"

Shinn hesitated. "The jacket will have to stay on.

But yes. I think that would be a good idea. We can bring him upstairs for a bit. The courtyard is secure."

"Excellent. And . . . well, there's something I have to tell you about your car."

When Shinn mentioned a courtyard, Tippicks assumed it was downstairs. Instead, while some beefy interns discussed how best to transport Harry, Shinn took him to the roof, to an open area covered with the metal net he'd seen from outside. It was pleasant enough, with benches and potted trees, but the crisscross shadows cast through the net lent the space a surreal air, making Tippicks feel as if he were in a giant bird cage.

Seeing Tippicks stare up, Shinn explained, "It's to prevent suicides."

"It's twenty feet up. Could someone really climb that high?"

"You'd be surprised what people are capable of," Shinn answered. He turned his head back toward the door. Harry was being led inside, flanked by interns. "Even with a ton of meds in them. *I* often am."

The interns walked Harry to a wooden bench, sat him down, then stood on either side of the only exit. Harry remained motionless, except for the slight rising and falling of his shoulders that indicated he was breathing.

Tippicks and Shinn walked over, Tippicks nearly tripping on his shoes as he went.

"Are you all right?"

"I'm having a bad day."

"Not as bad as our friend here, I hope." Shinn knelt gently by Harry's side. "Do you mind if I stay and listen, Mr. Keller?"

Harry nodded. "Pretty much."

"Okay. That's fine," Shinn said with a smile. "I have to call an auto body service anyway and send your teacher here the bill."

On his way out, Shinn squeezed Tippicks's arm and gave him a look, as if to say, *You must tell me everything.*

After that, except for the two interns who stood mutely at their posts, they were alone.

Tippicks sat on the far end of the bench, feeling how tired he was. The pain in his head had gathered toward the back of his skull, and though it wasn't quiet as bad as it had been, it still pounded steadily. He saw the grease still on his hand, looked at the tear in his tweed jacket, and wondered how much of the world was made up of accidents.

Steadying himself, he eyed the captive teen. "Harry, if you behave, they'll take the jacket off."

"Working on it," Harry said. He smiled at Tippicks. "Thanks for coming. Why, uh, did you come, by the way?"

Tippicks answered in a quiet voice, "Siara Warner came to see me yesterday."

Harry's eyes widened. Tippicks thought he saw a bit of that old spark flare in the dark of his pupils.

"She's all right? Was she with Jeremy Gronson?"

"Gronson? The football captain? No, she was alone," Tippicks said. He eyed the interns before continuing. They seemed more interested in whatever their iPods were playing. "But she did have a lot to say about you. And about time."

Harry's brow creased. "Siara . . . told you?"

Tippicks exhaled. "My father stayed here a few years. They didn't have this little courtyard back then."

He was surprised to see Harry nod. "Yeah, I know. He died here."

Tippicks eyed him. "How do you know that?"

"I saw it once, while I was looking at you. I can see people's . . . paths."

So the girl had been telling the truth, at least he couldn't what she'd heard. But could it really be . . . ? No, he couldn't go there yet. There was no proof of it.

"Harry, I was just a kid when my dad was here, but they let me visit him once or twice. Whenever I came, he told me the most amazing things, about all the places he'd gone, the *times* he'd seen, all over the world, all throughout history, without ever leaving his room."

Harry's brow knitted.

"But my mother and the doctors told me he was sick, crazy. So as much as I loved him, I never believed a word of what he said."

The lines in Harry's forehead went deeper. "Why?"

Tippicks smiled sadly. "Because I thought he was crazy, too, I guess. He went on about it, so much so they decided a lobotomy might help, but he died during the procedure. They poked a blood vessel in his brain by accident and couldn't stop the bleeding in time. As for me, well, as I grew older, I tried all the drugs I could, trying to see what he'd seen. And even though I never did, when Siara came to me, well . . . in a way, it seemed like another chance."

The lines in Harry's forehead went deeper still, surrounding his intent brown eyes with folded skin. Tippicks leaned in closer. "So, Mr. Keller, tell me, is it at all possible that it *is* true?"

Harry moved his head a bit, struggled to swallow. He licked his dry lips and stared Tippicks in the eyes. "Yeah, it's true. Well, I don't know about your father, exactly, but everything Siara told you is true."

To be sure, Tippicks repeated it as best he could remember, and Harry confirmed each detail, adding some of his own. By the end of it, Tippicks wasn't sure how much time had passed, or how much longer he'd have before Shinn returned, so he became a bit more hurried.

"Harry, the parallels are amazing, but—"

Harry sighed. "None of it's proof."

"Yes. Exactly. Is there anything you can predict? Anything you can show me?"

Harry shook his head. "Not now. The drugs keep me out."

"Siara said you took her there," Tippicks said. "Could you do that for me? Send me to A-Time?"

Harry shrugged. "Maybe. We could try. I might be able to talk you in, but I couldn't go with you, and it's dangerous."

Tippicks chuckled. "I grew up in the sixties. What could be more dangerous than that?"

"Okay. Umm . . . pick something to stare at."

Tippicks focused on a potted tree a few feet away. Some of the leaves were brown and dry, ready to fall off.

"Okay, got it."

As he stared at it, Harry spoke. His voice was slow, slurred, but there was a lilt to it, a droning, like he was reciting a poem or chanting:

"Look at the edges of the branches, the side of the pot, the color of the wall behind it. Keep staring."

Tippicks did as asked, but his head still hurt and the potted plant still looked just like a potted plant, no different than it had a second ago. Its edges vibrated a bit, but he was sure that was because he was so tired. How much had he slept in the last few days?

"Think about how all that—tree, branch, color, wall—how they're all just words."

Keller's voice droned on. It had a vague melody to it, something an awestruck girl like Siara Warner might think of as hypnotic, but it only irritated Tippicks, made him feel foolish. What was he doing encouraging this boy's delusions? What was he doing, trying to relive such an old pain at Harry Keller's expense?

". . . just lines your brain is making, they're all really part of one thing, part of the same thing, and you're really just imagining that there's any pot or tree or wall."

He should tell him to stop. He should apologize, to Harry, to Shinn. His behavior wasn't just unprofessional, it was inexcusable. His father had been the victim of a severe mental disorder, same as Harry Keller. He was just treading over old ground, trying to get blood from scar tissue. It was time to let go and grow up.

"Harry," he began.

He was about to say, "Stop" as gently as he could, when the edges of the brown leaves blurred into the wall. He was certain it was his failing eyesight, his headache, so he blinked, but the distortion only grew. His eyes were focused; he could feel it. It was the plant that blurred.

He felt a twinge, a strange fear, as the leaves pulsed green with life, then one by one turned brown and fell. At the same moment, the leaves grew smaller, receding into their stems, which flushed from brown to green, then wavered and shrank back into the soil.

What's happening?

He raised his hand to rub his head but felt his fingers still on his lap. He turned but saw his body remain behind. His head didn't hurt anymore. He'd left the pain behind. He wasn't in his body anymore. After knocking over two mugs of pens, scratching a BMW, and ripping his jacket, he saw himself tumble forward from the bench. Just another accident.

But there was nothing he could do about it.

The funny little fear grew. He felt himself pushed forward, as if he were being yanked up the highest hill on a roller coaster. For a moment, Tippicks paused on vertigo's brink, then plunged. Or rather, the world plunged around him, melting into a swirl of hypersaturated colors. Everything—Harry Keller, the plant, the walls, the interns, the tables, the great steel net above them—spread out into elongated trails.

In a flash, Emeril Tippicks stood atop those trails, watching impossible one-eyed beasts root about the land, while flat mandala patterns flitted about, weightless in a rainbow-colored sky. The world he knew had vanished, and with it the ancient doubts that had pressed upon his mind.

Whatever else he was, Jeffrey Tippicks was not *just* insane.

A solid tone filled his ears. Was it Keller's voice, still droning on, tethering him here? He turned about, trying to find the source, finally locating it on a small hill formed by thick trails that were intertwined like a giant's folded fingers. There was something in the air above them, a brightness, a light.

Was it Keller? Was he entering this A-Time, too, despite the drugs? No. Whatever it was, it glowed brighter and brighter, heating his skin in a comfortable, familiar way.

He took a few hesitant steps across the strange ground, trying to get closer, to see the light more clearly. And when he did, he gasped and said, "Dad?"

8.

"Help!" Harry cried. "I think he's having a heart attack!"

Like a sack of wet leaves, Tippicks's body tumbled forward. He looked like he was going to hit his head on the floor, hard. Unable to move his arms, Harry stuck his legs out to catch him. Tippicks's forehead hit Harry's shin and his chest slumped, his full weight falling on Harry's wobbly calves.

"Help!"

Harry knew what had happened. Tippicks had gone timeless alone. He prayed the guidance counselor would be all right. He had to be.

The two interns, cell phones in hand, raced toward them. They lifted Tippicks from Harry's legs and settled him on his back on the ground. He looked dead, but Harry realized this might be his one chance to escape. Even if Mr. Tippicks believed him, he'd never be able to get Harry out of Windfree so he could save Siara. The best the teacher could probably manage was to get himself fired.

As the interns bent over Tippicks's prone form, Harry bolted for the door. There were confused shouts behind him. Jesus and his friend didn't know who to deal with first, Tippicks or Harry. While they mulled it over, Harry put as much distance between himself and them as he could.

The drugs knocked him for a loop, but he was moving pretty fast for a guy in a straitjacket. Since his encounter with the Fool, nothing seemed to change his mental state much. He even had a brief A-Time flash of Jesus being fired for losing Harry twice. As it turned out, he soon got a better job at an alternative bookstore. After all, you can't keep Jesus down.

As he hit the door, Harry twisted sideways, praying they hadn't locked it. It opened, spilling him into the hall. He ran down the corridor, making turns as if he knew where he was going, a left, two rights, and into a stairwell. It was as if there was a voice in his head, whispering, *No, this way, not that way! Good! Faster! You're almost there!*

And there was. It was like the voice of the Quirkshard, only louder, and decidedly more helpful. Was it the Fool? Harry hadn't told Tippicks about the Fool, because he figured the whole giant-clown thing was just *too* weird. Whatever it was, it took him to the base of the stairs and through an emergency door, all without anyone spotting him.

An alarm shrieked as a blast of cold air hit him. He was facing a tall fence, eight feet at least, topped by barbed wire. Beyond that was a small forest of pines.

Go left!

He did, leaning against the chain-link for balance. The shrill alarm pierced his ears. After rounding a corner of the building, he spotted a section of fence that had been crushed by a fallen tree.

There!

He raced to the gap and nearly cut his face on the dangling coils of fallen barbed wire as he made his way to the other side. Another alarm went off closer, louder, angrier. He heard doors open. The field of tall, thin pines opened up in front of him. Maybe if he made it to the woods, he could find a place to hide.

Wait!

Wait? Wait for what?

Look!

Where?

A pink clown balloon, its string caught in the barbed wire, dangled in the air. A soft wind turned the face, the face of the Fool, toward him. Harry started, expecting the figure to speak, but instead, it graced the razor edge of the coil and popped.

Oh, he realized.

He turned and pushed the thick cloth of the straitjacket into the barbed wire, moving up and down. The thick cloth of one of the arms of the jacket caught and tore, exposing his flesh. It was the first time air had touched his arm for many, many hours, and the sensation made him shiver. He jammed the torn cloth against the barbed wire and pulled. This time, he managed to extend the rip all the way down his arm, scratching himself badly in the process.

Now, go!

Shredded cloth dangling down his side, he raced for the trees, snapping his hand out from the torn jacket as he moved. With one bare arm free he wasn't afraid of falling anymore, so he ran even faster. It wasn't like running in A-Time, where his breath never seemed to give out. Here the cold air hit his lungs hard, making it hard to breathe very deeply, and he hadn't eaten since he'd been in Windfree. He pushed his weakened body as hard as he could, but after a few minutes his legs went rubbery, and he wondered how long he had before he collapsed.

Already slowing, he came to a concrete drainage ditch, some sort of runoff, which he followed to a small tunnel of corrugated metal. A stream of water flowed in it, carrying bits of silt, twigs, and leaves. Harry knelt, crawled into the tunnel, and sat in the shallow stream. A final surge of energy, its source unknown, hit him, so he twisted, writhed, and tore at what was left of the straitjacket. Ten minutes later, he was out of it completely.

Shaking but satisfied, he lay back in the cool water, letting his arms dangle freely in the air. He rubbed his palms with his thumb, wriggled his fingers, scratched his scalp, and let the little stream roll over his shoulders and down his chest.

And Harry Keller exhaled and closed his eyes.

Alarms and sirens droned in the distance. He didn't hear any footsteps or rustling brush, no hint of danger, just the gurgling water as it flowed around him. He turned his head to look out the far side of the tunnel. Through the twisty curve of the metal's end he caught a glimpse of the nearby town of Billingham.

The horizon was a quiet one, with a ten-story building in the center, but nothing taller. If they didn't catch him, he could sneak into town, snag himself a shirt somewhere, and try to get on a bus back to the city.

But for right now, though the water was sharp and bracing, he had to rest. He closed his eyes, lowered his head and let the shallow coolness slosh around his ears. Then he passed into a long and dreamless sleep.

Thump! Thump!

Something hit Harry Keller's forehead. It wasn't hard, it wasn't heavy.

Thump! Thump!

It was hollow, rubbery.

Thump!

Like a balloon?

He opened his eyes, uncertain whether he was awake. The clown balloon was in the tunnel with him, floating over his head, thudding against him. It looked lifeless, like a printed illustration, but these days Harry was perfectly comfortable talking to inanimate objects.

"Did you . . . did you get me out of there?"

The picture of the clown smiled.

"Thanks," Harry said. He shuffled to a seated position, icy water running down his back. His pants were soaked.

He was shivering. He had a dull headache, but the numbness was missing. At least the cold bath seemed to have shaken some of the effects of the drugs out of him.

Harry looked out at the town. "I've got to stop whatever Jeremy's planning," he said to the balloon.

But the clown shook its head. "There's one thing you have to take care of first."

"What's that?"

The printed hand of the clown unfolded itself off the balloon. It swelled to human size and jutted a white-gloved index finger toward Harry's abdomen.

"That," the Fool said.

"What? You mean the Quirk-sha-ahhhhh!"

As the tip of the finger touched Harry's skin, he felt the shard writhe inside him. Strange, it was usually only in A-time that he felt the thing as a wound. In linear time, the shard manifested as that suicide voice in his head. He sure felt it as a wound now, though, twisting and turning in his cold skin like a piece of molten metal.

The bastard is changing the rules again!

Harry stumbled back, away from the finger, into the water. As he did, a red welt rose on his skin, right where the Quirk's claw had stabbed him. The white finger came forward again. Harry saw his skin sizzle as it touched the mark, and it didn't stop there. It kept pressing, harder and harder, until it went beneath the skin, probing into his gut, deeper and deeper, until finally, it seem to Harry that it touched the shard itself.

As a hot pain seared through his abdomen and into his brain, Harry could think only one thing: *It's going to pull it out! It's going to save me!*

But that's not what happened. Reaching the tip of the Quirk's buried claw, the finger didn't grab; it pushed.

The Fool didn't remove the shard. It pushed it further in.

"Ungh!" Harry cried.

Propelled by the white finger, the claw dug deeper into his gut, until it touched the tip of what Harry imagined was his spine.

Everything went black for a moment, then Harry bolted into a seated position, water dripping from his hair onto his shoulders. He looked at the far-off building, saw how high the sun was in the sky. What was it, late morning now? How long would it take him to get to Billingham?

The Fool had helped him. It had helped him indeed. There would be no more ambivalence. He would walk, he would run, he would get to where he needed to be, because now, at long last, Harry Keller knew exactly who he was and what he had to do.

He was a fool, a loser. And what he had to do was walk through the woods, go into town, find the nearest tall building, get to the top . . .

. . . and jump off.

So Harry Keller sloshed to his feet, left the tunnel, and started walking. A pink clown balloon followed, all on its own, as if it were a small dog nipping at his heels.

9. Once Siara stopped thanking Jeremy, the long drive grew quiet. She wanted to ask why he'd changed his mind, why he was doing her this ridiculously wonderful favor, but she was afraid that if she questioned it, it would vanish like a dream. So while he started playing his music, mostly house stuff, gangster rap, and a stray folk song or two, she made idle chat, only really brightening when she saw the white-and-green highway sign indicating they were three miles from Windfree/Billingham.

It was still morning. She could spend a few hours with Harry and be back in time for the demo easily. Things seemed to be going perfectly, until the sudden slowing of the car brought her attention back to Jeremy.

"Why are you stopping?"

"So I don't ram into all the cars in the traffic jam," he said, nodding toward his windshield.

She looked out as the car came to a halt behind a pickup truck. She could see the distant exit on the road ahead, but the cars were backed up for miles in both lanes. Sparse, bare trees lined the highway, but between them she caught a glimpse of police cars and an ambulance as they careened along the main road. A sudden *whoosh* made her cover her ears. Something low and loud passed directly over them, causing the entire car to vibrate.

Jeremy looked up as a shadow passed across the glass. "That's a police helicopter. Something big's going on."

A sinking feeling in Siara's heart told her that whatever it was, Harry was probably at the center of it.

"We'll never get there," she said.

Jeremy flicked on the radio and adjusted the tuner. "There must be a local news station. . . ."

A male voice came through the speakers. Courtesy of Jeremy's sound system it sounded full, lush, more real than any voice that Siara had ever heard.

". . . again, it is not known how he escaped, but apparently the patient has reached the roof of the Valis building and is threatening to jump off. The name is being withheld until family . . ."

Harry, Siara thought.

"Harry!" Siara screamed.

She knew about the Quirk-shard, but couldn't explain it to Jeremy. "He's tried to kill himself before!"

The town was just a few miles off. She reached for the

door handle, planning to run the whole way. But Jeremy's strong hand grabbed her wrist. His grip was cold, like a vise, and there was no crowbar handy this time.

"Jeremy, let me go! Now!"

He smiled. "No, wait. Stay."

"I can't. I've got to go find—"

His smile grew wider. "I know, I know. But this is a Humvee."

Before she could respond, he veered the huge car off the road. Soon they were racing past the trees, along farmland, past the traffic, toward the buildings. All the jostling nearly threw her from her seat.

"Are you crazy? They'll arrest us!" Siara shouted, but she had to admit she was excited by the ride.

"Don't think so. They seem busy with whatever else is going on," he answered, twisting his lips in a smug, boyish smile.

As the Humvee bounced up and down a few grassy hills and exploded onto a single-lane road, she realized it was true. The police cars and ambulances were all headed toward Billingham at top speed, straight toward the tallest thing visible, the ten-story structure she imagined must be the Valis building. Even from here she could make out the huge clock built into its center.

Hang on, Harry! she thought. *We're coming!*

Harry Keller was surprised at all the attention. Shirtless and wet, feet covered in the strange little sacks that passed for shoes at Windfree, he'd attracted a small crowd as he walked through the town. A police officer, some security guards, and even several pedestrians seemed to want to stop him, to help him, but every move they made was countered by a wild—one would think impossible—series of coincidences. Oranges flew from people's hands to trip them; cars lurched onto the sidewalk to cut them off.

Even more people began following him as he entered the town's prize centerpiece, the Valis building, and headed for the stairs, but their efforts were similarly thwarted.

Harry was touched. It was nice to know people cared so much about a stranger. But he also knew it was hopeless. The Quirk-shard was in total control of his steps, and the Fool was clearing the path.

And you really can't mess with a god.

Up the stairs, doors mysteriously locked behind him. Sprinklers went off. Alarms misfired, distracting anyone else who might have followed. By the time he reached the observation deck above the tower clock, he was alone.

Out on the street it had been cold. Up here it was freezing. Through the thin cloth on his feet, he soles felt numb, almost frostbitten. He felt a sick relief that soon it would be all over, that he wouldn't feel cold again, or anything else. He marched to the low wall that surrounded the deck and stepped up.

Standing there, on the brink, he felt the world as a rumbling rush above, below, and around him. Police cars screeched to a halt in the distant street. A nice ambulance was parked right in front of the building by a fire hydrant. All sorts of people in all sorts of uniforms rushed into the building. Even the doors to the observation deck flew open behind him.

"Don't do it!" a policeman screamed. He was an older man, white haired but fit, his face filled with genuine concern.

Ignore him! a voice inside him said. *Don't fear death, Harry! It'll be just like it was before you were born. And nothing hurt then, either, did it?*

The Quirk-shard made sense in a way, only there was one problem. Harry didn't really want to know what he felt like before he was born. Much as things had hurt, much as things had been frustrating, literally to the point of madness, he was still fond of living, still fond of the present. Besides which, Siara was out there somewhere, in the clutches of a major psycho, and Harry was the only one who knew.

Well, Mr. Tippicks knew, too, now, but who knew when he'd be back?

The clown balloon, having followed loyally all this time, rolled up the side of his leg and floated up in front of him. Harry wondered if anyone else could see it.

"It's okay, Harry," the clown on the balloon said. "You can jump."

Harry raised a single eyebrow, the way he'd seen Siara do a hundred times. It was the first time he'd ever managed it himself. "Easy for you to say. Balloons float."

The clown chuckled. "True, but you can float, too. Really. You just have to admit things don't make sense. Make the leap of faith your father never could and you'll fly! Points of entry are arbitrary. Let reason go, pick a partner, and dance."

It sounded good, so Harry raised a foot.

"Please!" the white-haired cop said. "Don't do it. The negotiator will be here in just a second and she'll know just what to say. Just wait a little while . . . please!"

No! We've waited so long! Just jump!

Tough choice. Who to believe?

Harry looked out at the world, at the tops of the buildings, the little people down below, connected by so many things, disconnected by so few. Subject to disease and war, one hand reaching for the stars, the other slinking back to the darkest cave. And all this time, he'd thought it had somehow all made sense, that he could figure it out.

But he was wrong.

"When you're right, you're right," he said to himself, to the Fool. "It doesn't make any sense. Not one bit."

He turned to look at the cop. "I'm really sorry about this," he said.

The cop lunged forward to grab him, but Harry smiled, shrugged, and let the Quirk-shard move his feet over the ledge.

Briefly, Harry felt weightless, just like he had so many years ago, trapped in his father's arms at the top of an amusement-park ride. There'd be no parachute this time, though. His stomach lurched. Everything spun. He was expecting to fly, but the Fool had lied. He wasn't flying. He was falling. It would all be over in seconds.

Thanks so, so much! the Quirk-shard said.

"Don't mention it," Harry answered, falling faster and faster.

Until he stopped.

Ow!

Ow? Ow? Just ow? Shouldn't I be squished or something?

Nope. He seemed to be floating. No parachute had opened above him, but the sidewalk loomed far below him and came no closer. He noticed a terrible pain in his crotch. Something hard and metal had caught the back of his pants and given him a humongous wedgie. A loud, hollow tick registered in his ears. He twisted to see the source.

The clock. His pants had somehow snagged on the minute hand of the tower clock. He was dangling from its center.

No! Not fair! the Quirk-shard whined.

The balloon floated up to his face and *thupped* him on the nose.

"Ha! Fooled you!" the Fool said.

"Yeah," Harry said. "Good one."

"So how you doing?"

Harry stared at it. "My gods are hallucinations, my faith insanity. You?"

The Fool shrugged. "Not so bad, really."

Harry's pants started to rip some more.

"This is only a reprieve, you know. Believe me, I've given you every possible chance. Think you can do it this time?"

"Uh . . . no. I'd really have to know what it is I'm supposed to do to do it."

Yay! the Quirk-shard thought.

The Fool shook its head. "Dummy. The rule of the Quirk is that you have to fall, right? But rules are meant to be bent. They're only masks, like everything else. See if you can figure out the rest."

The balloon *thupped* Harry one last time on the nose. The clown image smiled widely and vanished bit by bit, until only the twinkle in its eyes remained. Then that floated off among the clouds.

"Can I have another hint?" Harry called after it. It didn't answer. Nothing answered, save for the slight tearing sound as the thin cloth of his pants continued to give.

He felt the Quirk-shard in him, thrilled beyond belief, begging him to shred the last few inches of fabric himself and be done with it. He heard the giant clock behind him, droning out his last few seconds, *tick, tick, tick*, like Siara's poem about Sisyphus.

He looked again at the small city, the clouds, the sky, the buildings. Down below, the little people moved out in trails, ahead to their futures, back to their pasts. He even saw his own trail roll out in front of him, down to the ground, where his future body would go splat.

Funny, this was the first time he'd seen his own future. Maybe because it was so easy to see—after all, it only headed down. But it was still an A-Time vision, which meant the wacky side of his brain was coming back. Sort of. This was a halfway view. He saw the trails, but he saw the present, too, and they were superimposed on each other, looking like what they were, just masks. And masks were made to be removed.

He saw just where he would fall, what he would hit on the way down, and how he would die. He stared at the patterns for a while, sort of enjoying them, the way someone might appreciate a great painting; then he furrowed his brow one last time and said, "Oh. I get it."

He reached down, ripped his pants . . .

. . . and fell.

As the world rushed around him, faster and faster, he thought he heard someone screaming. At first he thought it might be him, but the voice was too high-pitched, too pained.

Siara. It sounded like Siara. Was she here? Was she watching? It didn't matter, really. It was all too late.

10. Siara and Jeremy drove to within a few blocks of the Valis building before the traffic forced them to park. Siara worried Jeremy might lose her on foot, but as they ran, adrenaline enabled her to keep pace with the high school football star. They raced along the sidewalk, but when that became too thick with people, they hit the street and sped between stopped cars.

Siara's heart hammered as she neared the police cordon and approached the mob gathered at its perimeter. She tried to push her way through, but couldn't. The mass formed a solid wall. With startling aggressiveness, Jeremy actually yanked some people out of the way, but even his efforts brought them only a few yards closer.

• As more curiosity-seekers pressed in to fill the void behind them, Siara found herself wedged so tightly in the crowd she couldn't breathe. Arms pinned, she noticed everyone was looking up, so she looked up, too. High up on the building, a half-naked figure was snagged on the minute hand of the massive clock, dangling from the seat of his pants like a stuffed toy or rag doll, a thing of cloth and stuffing instead of flesh and blood. The sight was so totally ridiculous, a pained laugh burst from her throat. It was Harry. At least he was alive; at least there was a chance someone would reach him.

But her strange smile soon vanished as she saw him tug at his pants, pull at the only thing keeping him alive, as if trying to tear himself free.

"No, Harry! Don't! Harry!" she cried. She hopped, still unable to move her arms. For a moment, he stopped his busywork. She thought he'd somehow heard her, but then he just fell.

Siara twisted her frail form against the thick, unyielding bodies that braced her, crazily thinking she might somehow catch him. As she struggled, all she said was, "Oh my God, oh my God, oh my God . . ."

The body of the strange boy Siara loved and sometimes thought she might be in love with plunged down the side of the building, turning in the air. Harry knocked against the stone siding hard and crashed into a flagpole, looking like a broken puppet. The pole flung him across the building's corner, where she just couldn't see him anymore.

As she stared at the empty spot where she'd seen him last, her hands reached out and squeezed Jeremy's arm so hard she was sure she must be hurting him.

"It wasn't his fault," she said, voice cracking. *The Daemon got him.*

"I know," Jeremy answered.

After that, she just kept screaming. The shocked but fascinated crowd rushed around the corner, hungry to see where the body landed. As the crowd thinned, she found she could move her arms again and breathe.

But she didn't want to.

So that was death, the consequence of time, as Harry had called it long ago. It wasn't anywhere near as magic or mythic as she'd once imagined, based on poems by Emily Dickinson (*"Because I could not stop for Death, he kindly stopped for me"*). It was too real, too gross, and too horribly, horribly ugly.

She found herself imagining the details, wondering if he'd broken his neck when he hit the building, if he'd suffocated on the way down, or if he'd still been alive for a moment after he'd hit bottom, living in a broken-up body. She wondered if it had hurt for long. She wondered if he'd been thinking of her.

Picturing Harry's body crushed from the fall, she thought of the two gerbils she had as a young girl for some reason, Beckett and Joyce, a mated pair. She always thought it was sweet, romantic that gerbils mated for life. But then Joyce grew sick and died and Beckett, rather than mourn her loss, ate her corpse. When Siara tried to stop him, Beckett, for the first time in his life, bit her, latching on to her index finger, burying his teeth deep inside her flesh, holding on so tightly she had to pry him off. Even now, years later, her finger tingled at the site the wound. She later read it was another gerbil instinct to eat their dead, to prevent predators from smelling the rotting body and attacking the nest.

So much for sentimentality. So much for gerbils.

Before Harry, that was the closest she'd come to death. Now *he* was dead. And her stomach twisted tighter than a gerbil's bite.

She vaguely felt Jeremy pull her through the police cordon. She heard him try to talk to the police, to explain who they were, how they knew Harry. They still weren't allowed any closer, not while the police recovered the body, which, they assured him, they didn't want to see anyway. She heard them say the remains would be at the hospital within an hour. If they really wanted to, Siara and Jeremy could talk to the doctors there.

Another hospital. Poor Harry was always in and out of hospitals, Siara thought; then she started to cry. Jeremy protectively wrapped himself around her, as if he were still her boyfriend, and walked them away from what remained of the crowd. They kept walking awhile, away from the Valis building. People still rushed by them, on their way to see what all the fuss was about, not realizing they'd missed it all.

A few blocks away, near where they'd parked, Jeremy found an old-style diner. It was nearly empty because of all the excitement outside, so he took her in. She slumped into a booth, felt a crack in the upholstery beneath her, and vaguely heard Jeremy ask a waitress for a cup of hot water.

The diner had chrome everywhere, and even where it wasn't chrome, it was shiny and silver: the counters, the tables, the knives and forks. It looked nothing like the dull little Formica diner back in Brenton, where she and Harry had had their only "date." Nothing at all. But it reminded her of it just the same. And it made her cry more.

The waitress brought a cup of hot water. Jeremy pulled a little packet from his pocket and sprinkled its contents into the cup. Siara watched as the tiny grains of something floated, tinting the water with tan swirls.

Tempests in a teacup.

"What's that?" Siara asked dully. She wiped her face with her arm. Realizing that wasn't enough to sop up the tears, she grabbed a napkin and blew her nose.

Jeremy shrugged. "Herbal tea. To help you relax."

She shook her head. "I don't want to relax. I want to be upset. Harry's . . ."

He pushed the cup toward her. "Take a sip. You've still got your mother's demo tonight."

She raised an eyebrow at him.

"I can't go there now," Siara said. "My mother wouldn't expect me to."

The steam from the tea rolled up into her nostrils. It had a spicy odor, like nutmeg. Jeremy gently lifted the cup and guided it up to her lips, like he was her dad or her big brother or something, and he wasn't going to take no for an answer. She didn't feel like fighting, so she took a sip.

The liquid, not too hot, slid down her throat. She could feel it warm her all the way down into her knotted stomach. She realized that, logically, the warm feeling should stop there, at the bottom of her stomach, but it didn't. It kept going down her legs into her toes; then it floated up her back , into her arms, even her fingers.

Everything started tingling. The knot loosened. Even the tingling where her pet had bit her finger vanished.

She blinked. She wasn't crying anymore.

"Finish it," Jeremy said. "It will help."

So she did. In a few moments, while the pain over Harry's death didn't stop exactly, it felt like it was floating away.

"What's in this?" she asked as she put the empty cup down. "Valerian root?"

"Something like that," Jeremy said. His face looked

115

so serious as it scanned her, so concerned, it made her smile. Why was she smiling? How could she smile when Harry was dead?

Something strong and warm tugged against her fingers. It took her a moment to realize Jeremy had taken her hands in his, cupped them, and pulled them toward the center of the table. She looked up into his steady blue eyes.

"It's important you keep busy now," he said in a funny sort of monotone. What a weird thing to say; again, like he was her dad or something, only her own dad would never say anything *that* dadlike. Shouldn't he talk about how awful it was to watch someone plunge to his death? How sorry he was? How he never really hated Harry, even though, of course, he did?

She tried to raise an eyebrow at him again but couldn't find the strength. Instead, she just said, "Yeah."

"So I think it's important that you still go to the demo tonight."

She hesitated, but his eyes and his voice were so much stronger than she was. Their certainty invaded her, like a poem, like the tea.

It made sense, in a way. Keep distracted, keep busy.

"Yes," she said.

"Your mother's been working so hard, there's no reason to upset her, not on her big night. So you really shouldn't mention what happened, right?"

That seemed a little funny, too, like it was dishonoring Harry. And how did Jeremy know how important the demo was to her mom?

But he seemed so sure, so she nodded. "Right."

He slipped a black iPod out of his pocket and put it in her hands. The plastic felt smooth and cool.

"What's this?" she asked. "A present? You know I can't see you anymore."

Her tongue felt sticky. Her voice drawled.

Jeremy smiled sweetly. "Just a distraction," he said. He placed its two earbuds in her ears. In a second, music filled her head, washing her, pounding her brain like it was the ocean and she was the sand. She didn't know the band, but she liked them. She looked at the box she held.

"Infinity in the palm of my hands," she said, quoting the Blake poem.

"Yes," Jeremy answered. "You might say that. But I liked the one you wrote about Sisyphus better. Remember that?"

Siara nodded, touched that he knew her little poem.

"I want you to listen to it, and keep listening to it."

"Sure," she said.

"Great," Jeremy said. "I'll drive you back to school then."

"Thanks," Siara answered. Her voice sounded dull and hollow, even to herself. So much so that she felt like she should apologize to Jeremy for not sounding more enthusiastic. She hoped he would understand, what with Harry being dead.

But death wasn't the only consequence of time.

As Harry Keller fell on purpose, he felt a pang, as if he were betraying his father by embracing a last-minute wildness. But he'd had not so much an idea as an intuition: *The Quirk says I have to fall, but it doesn't say how I have to fall.*

It was a crazy thought, logically impossible given the height of the building, but because Harry could see what would happen before it did, he also knew it could work.

So, as he tumbled by the eighth floor, he twisted his back just enough to make it slam into the side of the building.

Omph!

The impact felt like it had crushed his rib cage, but it did what he'd hoped; slowed his fall and changed his direction just enough for him to do a belly flop onto the sixth-floor flagpole. The pole had more give than the stone, but it stung like crazy all along his body in a long thick line that started at his navel and ended on his nose.

Ungh!

With the pole flipping him sideways, at least now he wasn't headed straight down. He was moving at an angle, away from the side of the building that faced the crowd, toward a huge, wide awning that hung over a fifth-floor balcony. It must be covering some sort of open-air restaurant he figured.

Anght!

He hit the cloth hard. Its thick canvas burned and bruised his bare skin as he slid along it. Thick though it was, the awning tore as he rolled, sending him off into the air again. He was in a wild spin now, out above a side street where a huge Thanksgiving banner stretched across the avenue. The next part would be tricky, especially with everything turning around and around.

He slammed into the banner.

YEOW!!

His still-spinning form stretched the thinner cloth on impact, suspending him against it briefly in midair, until gravity took effect and he started to fall again. With a second to spare, one of his flailing arms hooked the banner's edge. He grabbed the top of the banner in both hands and held on tight.

Urngk!

The strain felt like it would rip his arms out, but instead the weight of his body tore the banner off the steel cable that held it. Holding the cloth as it tore, Harry swung across the street, lower and lower. He was only thirty feet up now, still high enough to die.

As he made the Batman-like swing, he thought that if the crowd gathered at the front of the building could see him, they'd probably applaud. As it was, with everyone stuck in a mob at the main entrance of the Valis building, the only person who could see him was an old woman pushing a shopping cart, and she didn't seem to notice the ruckus going on right above the gray hairs of her head.

The swinging banner slammed him into a brick wall.

Ack!

Barely conscious, he lost his grip and tumbled, hit another awning, this one above a street-level pizza shop. He rolled off its edge to land with a splat on a pretzel cart.

Ulg!

The cart, owned and operated by a kindly man with a drinking problem, had not been well maintained. The rusty brake that held it in place often worked, but it had not been built to handle the impact of a flying Harry Keller. As a result, it loosened, and the cart wheeled off freely, taking Harry with it. Because he'd hit it at a bit of an angle, his remaining momentum gave the cart enough force to roll out into the street, where it hit the top of a hill, topped it, and headed down the other side, moving faster and faster.

The old woman finally noticed what was going on as Harry and the cart barreled past her. Before he rolled out of sight, Harry offered a weak wave, but she didn't seem interested in waving back.

Knowing what was next, he closed his eyes and

listened to the rumbling wheels beneath him. *Rumble-rumble-rumble-thuck!* A little sooner than expected, the cart slammed into the open back of a parked truck.

Urk!

But Harry didn't stop. He kept going, up and into the cargo bay, where he landed with a final thud in a huge pile of brown cardboard boxes. They fell on him, burying him, tearing, spilling their contents on his head.

When the driver approached, he didn't see Harry among all the cardboard, so he just sealed the doors. Moments later the truck pulled out.

As the smell of exhaust hit his nostrils, Harry moaned. His muscles throbbed. His bones ached. He was sure he'd broken at least a rib. But at least he knew exactly where he was and where he was headed. He was in the back of a truck belonging to a local practical-joke-supply manufacturer, headed back to the city. It would stop at a novelty store near RAW High School, bringing him round full circle.

A practical-joke-supply manufacturer. Coincidence, or a little wink from the Fool?

Both, Harry decided. Coincidence *was* the Fool. In fact, the whole fall, getting hit over and over, was like his conversation with the clown. It was also a lot like one of those old silent movies, with Harold Lloyd or Buster Keaton, where they'd bounce all over the place but still come out standing.

They *were Fools, too,* Harry realized.

In any case, he'd survived. He'd changed the rules. He'd seen enough of everything else's future that he'd finally glimpsed his own. If he were in A-Time now, he might even be able to enter his own trail.

There'd be plenty of time to find out about that. He had Siara and Jeremy to worry about first. And what about the Quirk-shard? It was being awfully quiet. Was it really gone?

As he lay in the back of the truck, struggling in a mess of fake doggie doo, plastic vomit, whoopee cushions and funny foam hats, he realized that for the first time in weeks, he was alone in his own head.

It was gone. He had fallen. The Quirk had happened. It was part of his life now, part of the past. And Harry Keller was still alive.

So far.

11. Eight miles high, the ebon thing quivered like a wrenching wound that defiled the sky. Black globs of bile spewed from its spreading cracks, falling in a sullen rain around the base, while all the rest oozed a sickly green putrescence. The Quirks didn't dare approach. They ran like dogs with tails between legs, even when they only touched its shadow. The otherwise inscrutable Timeflys tried to flap around and away from it, moving in flocks for protection. Those who flew too slowly were drawn in, pulled by an unseen force. One, after flapping frantically, gave up. As if tugged by a string, it glanced the edge of the tower and disintegrated in a flash, like an insect hitting a bug light, its pretty ashes joining the dark, wet rain. Seeing the fate of their comrade, the other Timeflys doubled their efforts to flee.

To most, the distorted column would seem grotesque. Even those who didn't believe in such things might call it a sin, but to the Initiate, to Jeremy Gronson, it was the coolest thing ever. And he had made it all himself.

Long dark robes fluttering, he strutted around it, ducking the falling globs, scanning every inch of every surface. Then he climbed up its side to check it all again close up. This piece worked, so did that. This one fit a little too tightly, but did it matter?

No.

Siara's future tunneled dead center into the thing. At the point of contact the colors of her life trail looked frail and faded, as if they too were being sucked inside. Her life twitched constantly, like a snake trying to pull its head from a too-tight hole, but it was trapped, hopelessly, permanently—thanks to the keystone.

A keystone. What a find that had been. What power. Keller never even guessed that he couldn't stop the warehouse fire because a keystone was in place. A-B-C-D. A is the keystone. If A happens, no power on earth can stop D.

Of course, Jeremy did have to use yet another special tea to get Siara into place, but why take any more risks? That tea was Jeremy's own brew, created after much research on the proper chemicals needed to bend a broken mind to his will. While she was under its influence, he might even be able to get her to make love to him, but what would be the point of that, with him where he was, inches from the goal line and nothing to block him anywhere in sight?

He looked up, pretending again to admire his work, but really just admiring himself.

I am here, I am here, I am here! he shouted in his mind. *Yeah!*

All at once, the timeless terrain beneath his feet rumbled. Jeremy shifted so it wouldn't catch him off balance, but he still found himself stumbling a few paces.

What was that?

Probably nothing. Or maybe an echo of all the potential energy his sculpture was building up. He'd need it. Every drop. He turned away from the malleable claylike future. Anyone could change that, really. The future was always being revised, even by the most humble decisions. Instead, Jeremy looked back at the vast, stony expanse of the past, where the colors were grayer but the shapes were stronger, more abstract, jutting from the barren landscape like a bizarre sculpture garden, every piece designed as a cautionary tale.

He who does not remember the past is condemned to repeat it.

What's past is past.

Water under the bridge.

Infinity in the palm of your hand . . .

My hand, Jeremy thought. *Mine.*

Hidden behind an elephantine lump in the trails, Harry Keller watched Jeremy Gronson's strange victory dance.

As predicted, the truck had deposited Harry a half mile from RAW. He could walk it in no time, but since the drugs no longer seemed to be stopping him, he figured it might be best to duck into an alley, take a quick trip into A-Time, and get the lay of the land. That was when he spotted Jeremy checking out the big ugly.

It was so strange to see him here in the trails. Sure, Harry had seen Siara and even Todd here, but they had a completely different feel to them, almost an aura that made them, to Harry's eyes, seem natural. He wondered if that was because they were here, as the Fool confirmed, on Harry's dime, using his words and thoughts to make the transcendental leap of consciousness.

Not Jeremy, though. His outline was crisp, sharp. It was almost as though he were pasted onto A-Time, like part of a collage.

Harry tensed and gritted his teeth the moment he saw him, wanting to race up and just have at him, but he held back. Being in A-Time made Harry feel more confident, but it seemed to turn Jeremy into some kind of predatory monster. He'd never looked stronger or more aggressive. A head-on fight was probably just what Jeremy wanted most, making it the one thing Harry should try hardest to avoid.

So Harry bit his tongue and watched and waited as the transcendent football captain circled the huge pillar twice more, then walked off and disappeared. Assuming the crazy man had gone back to linear time,

Harry stepped from his hiding spot and looked around at the vast Salvador Dalí topography.

The first thing he noticed was that the suicide-Quirk wasn't around anymore. It'd truly become part of Harry's own trail. Oddly enough, he hoped it was happy there. The second thing he noticed was that the future sky was darker than the rest, as if a storm were gathering there.

A light, cool breeze hit Harry's face. He'd never felt wind in A-Time before, either. Somehow feeling it now didn't seem like a good thing. And then there was that weird rumble, a cross between thunder and a slight earthquake, that even seemed to take Jeremy by surprise.

Why was Gronson messing with the future? What did he want? When Harry first stumbled onto A-Time, Todd was about to fire a gun at Jeremy. Obviously that was some kind of ruse. Jeremy had expected to be shot at—but why? And Melody, climbing atop the hospital, ready to gun people down with a high-powered rifle. It had to be Jeremy who'd placed the rifle there for her to find. Again, why? Harry couldn't imagine actually wanting to kill anyone. What did it mean for someone to want to see *scores* of people dead? What was the point?

It all has to do with this.

Eye narrowing, Harry approached the base of the thing. His scalp tingled as he came closer, as if the air around him were filled with the A-Time equivalent of static electricity. A few yards away, he stopped and craned his neck, attempting to see the top.

A hundred feet above him, another helpless Timefly hit the surface and disintegrated. Harry covered his face with his arm as a small shower of rainbow-colored soot tumbled along his jacket. At least he had some clothes on in A-Time. He wiped his face, blinked, and looked again.

At first it seemed that the only visible lines on the tower's surface were the oozing cracks. As he looked closer, though, he could make out, through the shades of black, the distorted, barely visible curves of life trails.

It was made out of the terrain, then. In fact, it was kind of like the knot of trails that led to the warehouse fire. The blackness of it, the way it leeched the color out of everything around it, seemed the same. But at the fire Harry had easily been able to see the individual strands, sort the threads. This was denser, more tightly wrapped. For all practical purposes, it was just one big mass.

Remembering the Timefly, Harry gingerly put his hand to it.

"Yeow!"

It burned. He yanked his hand back and looked at it. His palm had been seared off, revealing sinew and muscle beneath. The skin grew back quickly, the redness fading as he watched. It was damn strange to see. He shouldn't be so surprised; after all, he was made of

A-Time energy here, ergo, generated by his life trail. It wasn't real flesh or bone, exactly. Harry figured as long as his trail was okay, nothing here could hurt him forever, unless it affected his linear life.

But what had the sculpture done to that energy? And what was it doing to the timelines?

He circled slowly, retracing Jeremy's path, trying to sense what it was doing, or going to do. But he could get no impression from it other than a feeling of deep dread, as if he were in front of a nuclear bomb that was armed and ready to go off. As he made his way toward the part of the tower that faced the past, the dread thickened, but he didn't know why. There was something familiar, terribly familiar, nearby.

He spotted Siara's trail, stuck inside the thing, writhing, trying to free itself, and gulped.

I'm coming, Siara!

Without thinking, Harry dived atop the trail, put both hands on the surface, and tried to pull it free. No use. He tried to move his grasp closer to the section where her trail fed into the tower, but again the burning sensation came and his fingers began to melt.

This was not good, not good at all. He was breathing heavily, hyperventilating—*Can you do that in A-Time?*—scratching the side of his head as he looked. If he couldn't pull her free, maybe he could enter her trail, change something there, or at least figure out what was going to happen.

He recalled his vow not to enter her life trail, after accidentally seeing her take a shower. Then he remembered the Fool's words about changing the rules when you had to.

Sorry Siara, he thought as he dove inside.

The sensations that surrounded him were a breath of fresh air, especially compared to the rest of A-Time. Though it had only been a day or so since he'd seen her, it seemed like ages, and everything here, everything that rose from the walls, the ceiling, and floor, felt like her, as if she were standing right beside him. The friendly familiarity comforted him, relaxed him. Siara was more than just a crush, he realized; she was his only real friend since Carlton landed in the hospital, more like family than his own aunt. So he stood there a moment and just enjoyed the feeling before reminding himself that there were more important things to do.

As images rose from the stiff, curved walls, he realized he was still in the near past. He saw her fight with her father at their too-small kitchen table, felt her longing to go to Windfree, to help him.

I should get her something nice, he figured, moved by the scene.

When Jeremy appeared to pick her up in his Humvee, he was just a blur, his words garbled and unintelligible, just as they had been when Harry called him the Daemon. The title, Harry realized, was too dignified. He wished he'd chosen the Dick-wad or something more apropos.

He watched them drive together, saw them reach the Valis building, felt Siara try to move through the crowd. When he saw her collapse in tears, it dawned on him:

She thinks I'm dead!

Of course. Why wouldn't she? He wanted to rush back to linear time to show her he was okay, but he couldn't just yet, not until he found out what was going on. Unable to watch her grieve, he took a few quick steps toward the future. A chill filled the air and the walls grew darker. He was approaching the section of the trail that entered Jeremy's dark pillar, so he slowed and let the images rise once again.

It was that night, hours in the future. Siara was in RAW High School in the auditorium, wearing some sort of business suit, pushing a fruit cart down an aisle. The cart was topped with a huge banana.

What is this, Halloween again?

No, not quite. There was a lot of sleek equipment up on the stage. Something that looked sort of like a car engine sat on a pedestal, wires from it leading to a control panel. A few men in suits stood there, along with a woman who looked like an older version of Siara. Behind all that, almost behind the curtains, was a huge hydrogen tank.

Oh. Of course. The Peroxisome demo. Damn. I was supposed to do a paper on that.

Needing to understand more, Harry listened to the narrative voice that rose from the walls.

Pete Loam, her mother's boss, held aloft a small box only slightly bigger than the iPod in Siara's pocket. He was a funny guy, always buttoning and unbuttoning his dark jacket, as if never sure what the proper etiquette was. Sometimes he'd leave it unbuttoned as he stood and buttoned as he sat, which Siara thought was backward.

"Inside the vehicle," he said, unbuttoning, "the hydrogen will be stored in these small canisters, making the fuel cell vehicle literally as safe as one powered by gasoline. Safer, if you remember its only emissions are heat and water."

Then he buttoned his jacket again. Buttoned, unbuttoned. You could set your watch by him. Like Sisyphus.

As Pete droned on about how the hydrogen mixed with oxygen to produce the energy you'd need to propel a two-ton car, Siara pushed her fruit cart. It was piled high with apples, strawberries, and all the other healthy snacks her mother insisted on. The audience grabbed at her wares as she passed, but no one had touched the banana on top, which seemed a shame. It was so alone up there, balanced on top of the pile, aching to fall. It reminded her of Harry.

At the thought of him, she stopped pushing, rubbed her head and looked around. Nearly the whole school was here; teachers, too. Anyone who couldn't get a seat was probably out looking at the lobby displays or hanging around in the courtyard. After the warehouse fire, it seemed they all felt a need to cling together, to feel like one big thing, rather than a bunch of small, helpless ones.

Like Harry.

She felt a twinge, but the steady beat in her ears made it fade, so she pushed along again, handing out fruit and drinks, until Pete Loam buttoned his jacket and sat down, and her mother got up and said with a grin, "Let's get this party started."

With that, rather than just be embarrassed, Siara stopped handing out snacks and pushed the cart toward the front of the auditorium.

"Hey, Siara, nice outfit!" Jasmine called from an aisle seat. She was sitting next to Hutch and Dree near the front.

"How about a banana?" Dree asked cheerily.

Siara pushed past them, ignoring them, barely hearing Hutch's annoyed final whisper of "Hey! Take those damn earbuds out!"

She'd hurt their feelings, but didn't care. It was all about the music now. Being part of the moment, wanting whatever it was the moment would bring.

Just as the engine spun to life and the auditorium filled with applause, she abandoned the cart, grabbed the banana, and mounted the steps.

Siara was on the stage now, near the curtain's edge. She

looked at the clock, remembering the one Harry was stuck on before he fell, remembering the poem she'd written about Sisyphus as the minute hand, pushing up in one direction, falling back down forever, carrying not rocks but the burden of time.

It was 7:59, and the second hand swept toward twelve. The minute hand shivered and clicked into place. Eight o'clock. It was time.

She peeled the banana, took a bite, and started chewing. Most of the crowd was still applauding, but a few saw her eating and laughed. Her mother turned from the crowd, the smile fading from her face.

"Siara," she whispered. "What are you doing?"

"Siara!" her father hissed from the front row. "Get down! What is wrong with you?"

But her mouth was full, so she didn't answer.

More and more of the crowd were watching, not the engine, but her. Dree, Jasmine, and Hutch looked worried. Her mother looked frozen with shame. Her father was furious.

He leapt out of his seat and came up the side stairs. "Siara, stop this nonsense immediately!"

At about the same time, Pete Loam also saw her. He unbuttoned his jacket and came at her from the opposite direction.

"Excuse me, Miss."

She was done eating. All that was left was the peel. She reached out and dropped it just in time for her father to

134

step on it. He flew forward, slamming Pete Loam in the chest.

Loam's open jacket flared on either side of him, making him look like he had small but well-tailored wings as he sailed backward into the whirring engine. There were chugs and sparks as he hit. Tubes came loose and flew about like raging spaghetti.

Siara's father was just getting up, nose bloodied, when a single spark hit the end of one of the small canisters, igniting the hydrogen in it, and sending it sailing like a guided missile into the heart of the huge hydrogen tank. He didn't even have time to say his daughter's name one last time before everything exploded.

Harry pulled back. He wasn't sure where he was anymore; it was as if Siara had stopped being Siara, as if her entire being had somehow melted into this hideous event.

Images continued to assault him. The red flash grew white and hot, enveloping everyone in the auditorium. It blew outward, through the halls, the classrooms, the gym, heating the lockers so that the papers inside them, the hard work of the now-dead students, evaporated. It chased down the janitors, security, even the mice, until it reached the outer windows and blew them out, sending shards of glass into the courtyard and the surrounding street. But by then the explosion had weakened the beams that supported the center of the school, and the roof itself began to fold into the growing fire.

Harry heard a terrible wail, as if all the dying voices had joined together as one long moan. Then everything went black, black as the tower itself. A burning all over his body, on his arms, legs, torso, and head drove Harry back into the terrain, where he collapsed in a sullen heap.

He'd seen RAW High School destroyed, and everyone in it killed.

Reminding himself that none of what he'd seen had happened yet, Harry closed his eyes and tried to shake himself free of his grief. He'd seen Siara die once before, in an alley, but he'd saved her. He'd changed the future and saved her.

I can change this and save everyone. I can still change this.

He repeated it, over and over again, until his breathing slowed; then he opened his eyes. The unusual wind was whipping harder, slapping his mussed brown hair into his cheeks. The future sky was darker, its grayness beginning to complement the black of Jeremy's tower. The tower was changing, too; the cracks in it were elongating, giving off more of the vile ooze. The gray-green fluid stretched down along the huge shaft, into the ground and along the terrain.

The fissures in the past grew as the ooze spread into them. The ooze seeped along the crevices, down into every crack and cranny of the dried surface, where it sank and swelled and made even the adamantine surface of what-had-gone-before rumble.

The pressure built. The ground shook harder. If it kept growing that way, Harry worried that the past itself might yield and break.

"But that's impossible," Harry said aloud. "You can't change the past."

"Of course you can," a familiar voice behind him answered. "If you change the rules."

Harry whirled, expecting to see the Fool, but he didn't.

Instead, he saw Jeremy Gronson, standing just a few yards away.

12. It had been an hour since Siara's ex-boyfriend left her at the entrance of the modest apartments where she lived. They arrived at about the same time she'd would've been coming home from school. The timing was so perfect, he couldn't have planned it better.

Remembering Jeremy's words, those soft but powerful things repeated over and over during the course of the long drive, she went straight inside and locked herself in her room. As she sat on her bed staring at a wall, she barely noticed that her father hadn't installed the promised window locks. Dimly, she felt thankful.

She waited for time to pass, counting the seconds, the minutes. Occassionally the phone would ring. The machine would pick up and take a message.

"It's Dree! Why weren't you you-know-where today? Tell me what's up."

Hutch's voice was less friendly. "I demand an explanation, young lady."

Jasmine, who called last, just laughed nervously and said, "Oh . . . I wish you had a cell phone so I could leave you private messages! See you tonight?"

Part of her wanted to call back, to ask them for a hug, or to mourn for Harry with her, but instead she did as she was told. After exactly forty-three minutes, she dressed in the smart blue business skirt and jacket her mother had laid out for her. It was Peroxisome's official dress code, a wink of the eye from her mother to the corporate execs who'd be sure to see her that night.

Siara emerged from her room right on time to leave for the demo, the iPod earbuds firmly installed.

Seeing the buds, her father said, "Siara," in a disapproving tone.

"Must you?" her mother asked, finishing the thought. "Tonight?" But then she straightened Siara's jacket, swiped at the shoulders a few times, and kissed her on the cheek. "Never mind. Just thank you."

Her father sighed and rolled his eyes. Her parents said nothing more to her, chatting amiably to each other during the entire ride to school.

And not once—not once—did Siara ever even mention Harry or the fact that he was dead. It was okay. She was too busy listening to the music and looking forward to a time when the night would finally be over and she could stop being so obedient, stop wearing the monkey suit, stop being everything she hated so much.

"Think I'm a jackass? Think I wouldn't see you because you *hid*? The second I spotted your lame-ass trail, I knew you were still alive," Jeremy snarled. "Again."

He stood on a rise, glaring, black robes flowing around him like dark water. It was like he was posing or something, giving Harry a good long chance to appreciate how pissed off and scary he was. And he was both.

His A-Time form was as thick and muscular as his body in linear time, where he was the star jock of the school. In comparison, Harry wasn't exactly frail; he was . . . well, yeah, he was pretty frail compared to Jeremy Gronson.

What was really new to Harry was the unadulterated rage in Jeremy's eyes. In linear time, Jeremy had this wonder-boy thing going for him. Always the one with the gentle smile, the good-natured pat on the back. He only got angry when provoked, and why the hell would you want to do that? That was one reason Harry hated seeing Siara with him. It was like the guy was too good to be true.

Turned out, he was.

But here the alpha senior was gone, shed like a mask. (Hadn't the Fool said they were all masks?) The muscles in his jaw were tight with fury, twisting his face. Even the gleam in his eyes was different, as though a veil of compassion had been peeled away, letting the predator beneath show through all the more clearly.

The better to beat the crap out of you, my dear.

The A-Time wind, the wind that had never been there before, grew harsher. It whipped Jeremy's robes around, pushed his blond hair back, as if it were being angry right along with him, or rather, as if their anger was one in the same. And all of it, every ounce, was directed at Harry.

A dozen things to say to Jeremy, the guy who'd tried to kill him, the guy who was trying to kill everyone, flipped through Harry's mind: clever lunchroom comebacks, pointed commentary, insults, sarcasm. Among them:

Really? You saw my trail? That is so cool!

So, Gronson, what's up with the mass murder, dude?

Well, if you're so damn smart, then why am I still alive, huh, smart-ass?

You bastard, what have you done with Siara and, like, the world?

He also thought of screaming, *Hey, what's that behind you?* and running like hell in the opposite direction. But all those responses were useless, too ridiculous, so Harry settled on a look of total confusion and a single word that seemed to sum things up:

"Why?"

Jeremy's grin bared his teeth. "Like I'm going to

answer that, Keller? Like your cesspool brain would get it if I did? You think this is some stupid comic book? You the hero, me the villain?"

Harry looked at him there, standing in his black robe, planning to destroy the world, and shrugged. "Well, yeah, kinda. I mean, you *are* trying to kill all these people and I *am* trying to save them. Right?"

Jeremy's face shot past furious and squirmed to a whole new level of pissed. He spat as he screamed, "Shut up, Keller. Just shut up! You think you're so damn smart, don't you? Getting into A-Time—by accident! Screwing with my plans—by accident! You're just a pawn of the Masters! A puppet! A mask! You have no idea where you are, no idea what you've gotten into, no idea what I'm trying to do!"

Harry looked at the seething tower, then back at Jeremy. "Uh . . . trying to blow up the school and everyone in it, right? Kind of like . . . a comic-book villain?"

Jeremy screamed again and barreled toward Harry, shoving him with both hands. The moment his palms made contact, an intense vibration filled Harry's chest.

Harry flew backward, off his feet, onto his butt. Jeremy fell on him, knocking him back to the ground, then holding him down with his knees.

When he grabbed Harry's skull in his powerful hands and squeezed, the vibrations intensified. They weren't just on the surface of his head, they were working their way in, as if pushing pieces of whatever he was made of in A-Time out of the way, drilling deeper and deeper. It was a familiar feeling, like the one he had whenever he entered his own trail, just before he was hurled out.

The azure coals of Jeremy's eyes likewise bored into his brain. "Now *I* get to ask why, and the difference is *I'm* going to find out."

Jeremy's hands squeezed tighter. His long middle fingers pressed the top of Harry's skull, drilling past his hair to the scalp. His thumbs wedged themselves at the joint of Harry's jaw. If Harry had been in his trail, the force would have ejected him, high into the A-Time sky, but here he was pinned.

"How did you survive? How?"

"You . . . could've . . . just . . . asked . . . ," Harry said.

Harry's arms flailed impotently at Jeremy, his hands trying to pull the thick tree-trunks of his arms away. Beads of sweat appeared on Jeremy's flat forehead. They pooled and ran in rivulets, falling on Harry's face in thick salty drops.

"Peh!" Harry said, spitting and twitching. "That is so gross."

Jeremy's brow furrowed. He looked confused. "How can you stand to be what you are? It's so chaotic, so uncertain, so inept, so impossible."

The burrowing vibrations hit the back of Harry's

head and seemed crash out into the ground under him. Jeremy inhaled sharply. His face shivered, his grip relaxed. At first he seemed to understand something, but then the look of confusion deepened.

"The Masters didn't help you. A clown? A clown saved you? It said it was a god and you believed it? Why would a god come to you and not me? That doesn't make any sense!" he screamed.

And everything has to make sense.

His grip tightened again, sending new waves of pain into Harry's skull, increasing the intensity of the reverberations until Harry thought he would burst. Despite the pain—which he was starting to get used to, after the beating the Fool gave him—he realized Jeremy was reading Harry's past the same way Harry read trails, only through his fingers somehow.

Why not? They weren't physical here; they were A-Time energy, ergo, generated by their life trails. *Jeremy must know how to follow the energy back to the trail and read it.*

"There must be some other answer!" Jeremy wailed. He was getting tired, as if the strain of touching Harry was too much. Now why would that be?

"The vibrations," Harry realized. "You're . . . feeling them, too . . . aren't you?"

A flash of panic in Jeremy's eyes told him he was right.

And if that's mutual, if you can read me, maybe I can read you!

Harry lifted his hands and imitated Jeremy, wrapping his own fingers around Jeremy's thick skull. Jeremy looked vulnerable for a moment as he quivered and growled.

"No!"

The moment was short-lived. Jeremy recovered, pulled Harry's hands away, rose, and kicked him in the side, but it was too late. Harry had held on long enough to yank something free from the power-mad jock.

Images flooded Harry's head, whole hog, like the way the Fool spoke. Now it was just a question of sorting out the details. He snatched at a vision and focused. A beautiful young couple, well dressed, hopeful yet somehow severe, sat in a doctor's office awaiting his word. To Harry's surprise, a narrative voice rose, just like in the trails:

> Finally, the doctor picked his head up from the clipboard and spoke. "It's not only that it hasn't been done before, it's that I'm not sure it should be. Many of my colleagues would question the ethics of selecting a particular fertilized egg on the basis of its genetics. Should we really be in the business of judging a human life because of its potential IQ or how strong it might be?"
>
> The woman's eyes narrowed sharply, deep and blue. "Since when is it unethical to strive for the best?"
>
> Her husband sneered. "Besides, we're paying you enough."
>
> The doctor grimaced.
>
> The woman's features softened. She reached out and

took the doctor's hand in her long fingers, catching him with her eyes. "Please, we've already lost one child."

The doctor met her gaze. "And even though it was two years ago, it's clear you're still traumatized by the car accident, not thinking clearly. You can't expect perfection out of life. It's not that kind of thing."

The husband shook his head. "Of course we can. We've given up the drugs completely. Turned our life around. Now we only settle for the best."

The woman smiled, adding, "And we only drink tea."

Red lightning flashes played on Harry's inner eye. He saw dozens of healthy embryos rejected before the Gronsons settled on the one they loved best. The day it was planted in her womb they named it Jeremy, and set about planning the rest of Jeremy's perfect life.

The baby was born after ten months' gestation. They had to puncture the embryonic sac with a long thin needle to induce labor. He was born overweight, with a thick shock of blond hair. He didn't cry; he just glared at everything, as if the world were a nuisance.

"He has your eyes," Mrs. Gronson said.

"He's going to be a scientist," Mr. Gronson said.

"An artist," Mrs. Gronson answered.

"We'll make him both."

They were like Harry's dad in a way, accepting no less than perfection from their son. But their motives were different. Frank Keller wanted to defeat death in the name of his deceased wife, but the Gronsons wanted to win at life, as if it were some sort of game.

Jeremy's life accelerated, speeding by too quickly for Harry to follow. In the broken mirror shards that shimmered around him, he saw a parade of tutors. One, in particular, glowed sharply. Harry shuddered as the man came to meet Mr. Gronson in his Wall Street office.

Mr. Dan Chabbers was so lean that the skin on his face and skull sagged and had an unhealthy glow. When he tried to smile, even politely, his long teeth, slightly yellow, made him look like a ghoul. Gronson hated speaking to him, but the man's reputation for achieving remarkable results in behavior modification preceded him. He was the best.

"So what are you saying? He's not going to be a chess champion by the time he's six, as you promised?"

Chabbers shook his head. "No, I'm not saying that at all. I'm no genetic expert, so I don't pretend to know where these traits come from, but he's very rigid. Couple that with the natural energy all boys have at his age and you have a terrific source of . . . resistance."

Gronson rapped his fingers on his desk. "I'm not paying you to tell me what my son is. I'm paying you to make him the best. Are you saying you can't do it?"

Chabbers gave him that long-toothed smile. "Of course I can, but to meet his resistance, I need to be able to show the boy that I am the greater force. That I am the master. This requires, on occasion, corporal punishment, which in this state is technically illegal. But free my

147

hands and I can assure you your child will become quite exceptional. . . ."

Gronson exhaled through his nostrils like a bull and rapped his fingers on the desk again, as if they were his hooves.

"Just do it."

"As you like, sir. And trust me, you're doing the right thing. When I'm done with him, he will not simply believe he cannot fail—he will be convinced he's not allowed to."

"You think you can touch me? You think you can see my life? The joke's on you, Keller. The joke *is* you, Keller. None of that matters. None of that is me!" Jeremy said.

Dizzied by the visions, Harry didn't even block as Jeremy punched him, he just fell. A flurry of hard kicks followed. The pain was so overwhelming, it made Harry want to give up. The only thing that kept him going was something the Fool had said: Asking questions in a way that got him beat up was part of Harry's character. This just seemed like more of the same.

The phantasms were fading, but Harry clearly witnessed Jeremy's trip to France, saw him find the herbs, translate the strange instructions, and enter A-Time. There, he appeared as an indistinguishable blur, just as Harry had seen him when he called him the Daemon. But then, to Harry's shock, the timeless football jock encountered not only Quirks and Timeflys, but a bunch of *other* blurs.

Other blurs. Other A-Time travelers.

He remembered what Jeremy had said about Masters, and realized he wasn't talking about his sadistic tutor. Through the pain, Harry spoke out in surprise.

"There's . . . *lots* of us? A group? Obscure Masters?"

Jeremy didn't answer, he just sprang at him, full body, but he was tired, and Harry managed to roll out of the way and stumble to his feet.

Having his past sucked from him drained him as much as it did me. Maybe if I let him kill *me, he'll get really tired.*

Harry wanted more answers. Realizing Jeremy wasn't going to offer any, he parsed the shimmering, fading pictures that remained in his head, fast and furious. The Obscure Masters were an elite club, so naturally Jeremy felt he had to join. He was given a task to prove his worth. It centered on the quatrain by Nostradamus that he'd found in France:

In the year 1999, in the seventh month, from the sky will come the great King of Terror, bringing back to life the great King of the Mongols. Before and after, Mars to reign by good fortune.

From what Harry could gather, the quatrain was *supposed* to be about World War III. In the early nineties, a US general pushed a plan to capture the oil fields of Saudi Arabia, to secure the energy supply. The resulting rebellion in the Middle East would have led to Iran and Iraq not just developing nuclear bombs, but using them, leading to a war in 1999 that left many, many dead. Mars being the god of war.

It was the stuff of a bad science-fiction movie, but Jeremy believed.

There was a grunt behind him. Jeremy charged again, but Harry ducked him easily, and the tired alpha male found himself eating trail. The images were almost gone, but Harry was still able to make sense out of them.

Something unexpected happened next, something good. Because of a breakthrough in fuel cell technology that opened the possibility for a new type of engine, the administration saw another way out. The invasion plan was scuttled. The future changed. WW III did not occur and Nostradamus, despite being dead for hundreds of years, was embarrassed. It became Jeremy's initiation task, then, to make sure the prophecy occurred by somehow changing the past. Of course, they didn't tell him how to do that.

Even Harry could see the whole idea was totally, absolutely, completely, insane, a sick joke at best, but Jeremy threw himself at it with byzantine gusto, warping events in the intricate, callous ways only a genetically bred psychotic could.

The images shrank into wisps. Harry struggled to snatch at them, straining to see Todd Penderwhistle sitting in the school auditorium. He raised his gun to fire at Jeremy, but here things happened the way Jeremy *wanted*. Todd fired. Jeremy ducked. Before he could drop the gun or run, Todd was rushed by Jeremy's football pals. Panicked, he turned the weapon on them, firing, at one, two, three, marveling at how the muscular teens were dropped by the small pieces of lead. There were seven dead before Todd remembered they were people, then turned the gun on himself and made it an even eight.

So Harry hadn't saved *Jeremy* from Todd, he'd saved a bunch of other people, mostly Jeremy's teammates. Next, Jeremy tried turning Melody into a random shooter. Finally, he tried frying the senior class in the warehouse fire.

But somewhere along the way, from Quirk to Glitch to fire, Jeremy's methods had drastically improved. When Harry tried to stop the fire before it happened, the future changed back on its own, as if it was inevitable. The last vision evaporated before Harry could see why.

The images gone, he turned back to the red-faced, exhausted Jeremy.

"A keystone? What the hell is that, Jeremy? Tell me!"

Jeremy leveled his eyes at him, his chest heaving. "If I do, if I tell you, will you promise to just *die* right after that?"

"Uh . . . no?"

"Then forget it!" Jeremy growled, pulled back his strong arms, spread his fingers, and came forward. Anyone else might have tried to block the coming blows, but not Harry, not this time. Wanting the whole story, he came forward, too. Just before Jeremy reached him, Harry dug his fingers into the rugged flesh of Jeremy's face. Though Harry's fingers weren't nearly as long or strong, Jeremy shrieked and his eyes went wide.

Harry held tightly as the intense energy passed between them. In seconds, Jeremy maneuvered his arms between Harry's and slammed him away, but not before Harry had found what he wanted.

A keystone event.

It was kind of like the butterfly effect, where the flapping wings of a butterfly can set in motion a chain of events that eventually cause a hurricane thousands of miles away. Sensitive dependence on initial conditions. A butterfly flaps its wings, changing the wind just slightly, so the next wind changes a little more, the next even more, and so on, until you have something being tracked by radar and named after a woman.

In the time trails, the keystone could be anything—say, someone opening a page in a book—but at the warehouse, it had worked kinda like this:

a. While two seniors painted a giant spider for the party, the paint spilled.

b. One went to get more paint and wound up flirting with a cashier.

c. His miffed pal left for the party without him.

d. At the warehouse, said pal didn't tie the rope that

held the spider as tightly as his friend would have.

e. During the party, the rope came lose and the arachnid swung into a light pole.

f. The light pole fell, sending its sizzling wires flailing every which way.

g. One wire hit the spare gasoline can being kept for the generator.

h. Boom!

Now, if (a.) is the keystone, you can stop the paint can from spilling easily; but if you don't, and it spills, nothing on heaven or earth can stop (h.). That was why Harry couldn't keep any students from attending the warehouse party, no matter how hard he tried.

The events leading to the explosion at RAW had another keystone, but what was it? What simple, stupid little thing did Harry have to stop, to save Siara and the school? Should be easy enough to figure out . . .

Wham!

Though his eyesight was blurred, Harry saw that Jeremy, apparently not as dazed as he looked, had hit him in the side of the head with a piece of the terrain, sending him sideways and to the ground. The clunky club was so big, it nearly took Jeremy off his feet as he swung. As for Harry, it not only hurt, it also sent all those images swirling like white spots in a shaken snow globe. His arm looked as if portions of it had been torn away.

"Touchdown for Gronson!" Jeremy howled. Then he stood, one foot on either side of Harry. He swung the terrain over his head. "And now I'm going to smash the old pigskin down . . . on your skull."

"You stupid jock!" Harry shouted. "It's not a game! It's people! How can you do all this just to join some stupid club?"

Jeremy's lips curled in disdain. "Siara? Why should that artsy-fartsy bitch be special? Think I love her? I'll tell you something you'll never understand. It'll be like speaking Latin to a dog. If I did love her, it'd only make me enjoy her death more."

"You're right. I don't understand. For the first time, I don't even think I want to."

"Told you." He tightened his grip again.

Harry tried to think of something to say or do that might delay the next blow, but as he did, before the blizzard of images in his head rushed off into oblivion, a final picture formed that made Jeremy's attitude toward most human life seem like a minor sin.

"You *killed* your own parents?"

"Yes. Yes, I did."

He said it as if he were reminding himself, then stopped cold. He panted. He wavered on his feet. He even lowered the club a bit. His mouth was still grinning—leering, really—but his eyes looked scared, as if they were horrified by what the rest of his body had done.

"Only it wasn't killing. The self is an illusion. So *they* were illusions, illusions that held me back, tied me

154

to a false world with masks. This, this is the real game, Keller, what you call A-Time. I needed to see that completely, sever all my ties, clear my path to success. Any attachment to that world only held me back."

For a moment, Jeremy looked sad, as if part of him had really wanted to be held back, just once. He let the club fall to the ground, held its tip loosely in one hand.

"Jeremy, did the Obscure Masters tell you all that?" Harry asked.

"Not in so many words. Mostly I figured it out myself. Just like I figured out the keystone, like I figured out how to change the past, like I'm going to figure out how to destroy you."

Seeing the pain still swimming in Jeremy's eyes, realizing he was vulnerable, Harry tried another question.

"How can killing all those people change the past?"

Jeremy pounded his fist into his open hand and answered through clenched teeth. "I just told you! They're not people! They're energy, bound up in disgusting, fake little selves. Crack them and you can absorb it, direct it, channel it. My sculpture directs it into the past."

"And what happens then?" Harry asked. "What happens if you get your war, you win your last trophy, and you join your Masters?"

"Then? I'll be finished, Keller. Finally finished," Jeremy said wistfully. Harry caught a glimpse of the deep exhaustion in the alpha boy's eyes. "I'll be able to do anything, even bring them all back, just as toys, while I live forever in the only real there is. No pain, no gain, no death . . ."

Realizing something, Jeremy snapped his fingers. "That's it! That's it! You're here. *You* know the trails. *You* live forever, too. Heh. Wait a minute, wait a minute. Oh, this is going to be good. I can feel it."

Jeremy scratched his chin and looked off. "Crack them. Crack them open. I've been going about it all wrong." He wagged his finger. "But now I think I've finally figured out exactly how to kill you."

Harry watched aghast as Jeremy turned away and walked off.

"Jeremy? Wait. Where are you going, Jeremy?"

But Jeremy ignored him, chuckling as he marched. "Nothing dies here, Keller. Except maybe you . . ."

13. The auditorium lights were low, casting the student body in shades of brown and gray so that the people, the chairs, and the carpet all melted together, a little like the A-Time rush Harry had once given Siara. Standing there, watching dully, she remembered how she'd once wondered if it was just that rush of transcending time that attracted her to Harry.

Now that he was gone, though, she knew for certain that A-Time was still out there somewhere, and it was Harry alone she missed.

"Honey?" Siara's father said, waving his hands in front of her eyes. "Earth to Siara? Come in, Siara?"

She pointed to the earbuds and waved her fingers,

indicating she was pretending not to hear him.

"You sure you're all right?" he father asked. "Anything you want to talk about?"

The auditorium clock was right above his head, looking like a black-and-white bubble rising from his shiny bald spot. It said, in its limited language of tick-tocks, lines, and numbers, 7:38. Only about twenty minutes to go before they started the engine.

Dad sighed, mouthed, "Whatever," and trudged to his reserved seat in the front row. She watched as he gracefully adjusted his favorite tie, wanting to look his best for his wife's big night. As she did, Siara felt like she was staring at an old picture of something she'd been part of once, back when she was a child.

Emotions, angry at being forgotten, welled like a tsunami, ready to wash her away. Like every time before, though, just as the feelings were about to crest, to speak, they receded, sucked back into themselves, into nothing.

She watched her father waiting patiently with his hands folded on his lap and couldn't find the part of herself that cared about him. Her mother was on stage, sitting in a folding chair along with about six suits from her company. She looked nervous. Siara briefly felt bad for her, but it passed, and she started seeming further and further away.

When the clock hit 7:39, she pressed play on the iPod and let Jeremy's music fill her ears.

Forget about it
Forget it all
Just find the wheels
And do as you were told

The music was a bit too much like techno-pop for her tastes, but it had a steady beat. She gave herself over to it, embracing the distraction with her disaffection. Free from all her feelings, free to obey, she headed for the silver food cart her mother wanted her to push around.

"Hey, Siara," a rough voice said. A guy with curly red hair gave her a goofy smile. She knew him from math or someplace and should have said hello, but she just walked right past him. He mumbled some lame joke about her outfit as she passed. Or was it a compliment?

The cart was in the corner, past the auditorium doors. She pulled it free, ready to forget about it all and do as she was told. It jostled as she pushed it over the rubber strips the AV kids used to cover the wires. Juice sloshed in bottles. The banana that topped the fruit bowl shifted slightly, curving across an apple. For a moment, she thought it might fall, like a pen off a desk, or a body from a building, but it didn't. It somehow held on.

Keep it up, keep it rolling
Do as you were told

As she reached the middle rows she saw Jasmine,

Dree, and Hutch. As she watched them gabbing, laughing, checking out the hot boys, she felt another pang, a longing to go to them. The tsunami of disenfranchised feeling welled again, but the volume on the song rose to meet it, all on its own, like a great sandbag wall of sound. And though she'd known Jasmine, Hutch, and Dree since grade school, she soon couldn't find the part of herself that cared about them, either. It was like they were all just . . . bad ideas she'd had once, ideas she hadn't even bothered to write down.

Ignore everything else
It's not important anymore
Just do as you were told

Sure, it was overproduced. The synthetic drums and strange trilling noises were annoying, and the lyrics were stupid and monotonous, but the melody was really working for her. Funny how it wasn't like poetry. Poetry connected her to the world. This just yanked all the wires out.

She rolled the cart down the aisle. Hands reached and grabbed at the free juice and fruit. Something inside her told her she should be mortified, at least embarrassed to be standing here in a corporate costume handing out fruit instead of being zombie Emily Dickinson. That was some other Siara, another bad idea she'd forgotten.

The house lights went even dimmer and the stage lit up like the sun. Showtime. With fewer students grabbing from the cart, she easily pushed it toward the front row, near where her father sat. The floor dipped and rolled down there, so she had to pull back now and then to keep it from rolling off out of control, like it was a horse or something.

Someone in a suit was talking, but she couldn't make out what he was saying. The music in her ears had gotten louder, its beat infecting her blood, staining it:

Get up on the stage, Siara
Take the banana with you
Do as you were told
And you can see Harry again

Ha. Music had spoken to her before, but this was ridiculous. *Okay, lousy song. If that's the case,* Siara figured, *I'd better get on with it.*

Wouldn't want to keep Harry waiting.

"Jeremy? Yo, Jeremy? Yo! Where are you going? What are doing? What's up, dude?" Harry asked, scrambling after him.

Jeremy trudged off along the terrain, happy and full of purpose.

"You'll see, Keller. It's a surprise."

Feeling deeply worried but having no idea why, Harry debated trying to tackle him, but before he could, the ground wobbled beneath his feet.

And what the hell is this?

It was like he was standing on a water bed. The

trails were trembling en masse, the disturbances centered on Jeremy's thing. If that wasn't enough, the event horizon, the sizzling line that phased future into past, was nearing the tower. It wouldn't be long before it hit—and what would happen then? WW III?

All the while, the snowballing changes in the landscape seemed to matter little to the Initiate as he continued on his path, still smiling.

Flustered, out of ideas, Harry ran and jumped Jeremy from behind. Normally, he wouldn't have been heavy enough to take down the quarterback, but as Harry hit Jeremy and wrapped his arms around his neck, the terrain shifted again and they both tumbled to the ground. No soonder did he land then Jeremy, almost calmly, kicked Harry with both feet, sending him scuttling across the landscape. By the time Harry skidded to a halt, Jeremy was standing again.

"Oh, give it up, will you? Making a mistake I can deal with. I can fix it and move on. But you, Keller, you're like a little piece of hot dog in my stomach that just won't digest."

"Have you tried antacid?"

Jeremy didn't answer. He just jumped across the twisting trails, scooped Harry into the air, and spun. Harry felt his body whirl, saw A-Time blend into a kaleidoscopic haze. He punched at the powerful hands that held him, slamming his knuckles into the backs of Jeremy's hands, making him let go. As he sailed into the

A-Time air, Harry could hear the annoyed gurgle in Jeremy's throat as he flew toward Jeremy's great big Thing of Death.

Harry didn't hit it, he just skimmed the side, but his skin burned where he touched it. He landed at the tower's base, where Siara's trail entered. Her life felt warm, reassuring, as close to a pillow as A-Time terrain could get. It pained him to see it writhing, trying to earn its freedom from its Jeremy-intended future.

As the Initiate maneuvered the gyrating trails to reach him, Harry stuck his hands into Siara's life and again tried to pull it away. Unable to guess at what the keystone could be, he tried changing everything he could think of—timing, outfits, phone calls, traffic lights—but her life remained lodged firm and fast in the base of the thing, and could not be moved.

It was futile.

Jeremy was coming, so Harry stuck his head and shoulders in. He could make out the stage with the big hydrogen tank and the sleek metal-and-plastic display engine. He saw Siara pushing her cart, listening to Jeremy's hypnotic words on her earbuds.

Fake world or not, he's not just working from A-Time, Harry realized. *He's covering all his bets.*

Before he could see anything else, Jeremy grabbed him by the feet and pulled. Harry grabbed at the tunnel walls, trying to keep himself in, and the two tugged back and forth. Harry's hands scrambled for a hold, his arms ached with the strain, but he held on until he heard a horrible sound, a sound he would always remember but never, ever be able to describe.

He turned his head toward Siara's future, saw where her life entered the tower, and felt a cold, horrid wind, a total blackness that made him wonder if maybe changing the past would do something screwy to *everyone's* filters, if maybe time really would just . . . end.

He gasped and let go. Jeremy yanked him up immediately.

Now Harry lay on his back, his ankles in Jeremy's hands. The sky was dark, darker then he'd ever seen a sky, and the terrain utterly barren. If he was going to do something, it would have to be soon.

Unable to think of anything else, he screamed. "Look around you, you quantum pedantic! Your sick-ass plan just shot past psycho and into something else entirely! All the Quirks are gone! The Timeflys, too! Look at the cracks! Look at the sky!"

From the look on Jeremy's face, Harry thought he might be getting through. He let go of Harry, rolled his shoulders, and looked around. There were flashes of something like lightning centering around the tower, and a sound like rolling thunder, only rather than a low, steady boom, it sounded more like some great beast, its voice deeper than an ocean, weeping.

Jeremy shrugged. "So maybe I got some details wrong. I'll fix it later. But not before I take care of you!"

Harry shook his head is disbelief. He stood, pulled back, and punched Jeremy square in the jaw. Shocked by the bold frontal assault, Jeremy staggered backwards.

"Then come and get me, asshole," Harry said.

And he waited for Jeremy to charge.

Heeding the heavy force of gravity, the cart pulled forward, against Siara's will. Its nature made it want to roll down the aisle and smash into the side of the stage, to spill and make a mess of itself, but she wouldn't let it, insisting instead that it do as it was told. As the speeches and introductions filled the hall, she chose to keep the cart in control, to make it *walk* when it wanted to run.

Like yesterday, when her father held her back from seeing Harry. No, that wasn't fair. It wasn't really her father, was it? The window was open and he was in the kitchen. She could have dived out into the street and hitched. Then she would have made it there, maybe in time to save him. So it wasn't her father who stopped her, or Jeremy, either. It was herself. Trapped between two worlds, she'd chosen neither and just let things happen. Hers were the hands that held back her own rolling fruit cart of a life.

Was that what growing up was about? Getting to a place where you felt like you couldn't make choices anymore? Like her dad working a job he hated for decades, to keep a roof over his family, only to have his daughter disappoint him?

How could that possibly ever be worth it if, in the end, like Harry, you only died anyway?

She opened her hands slightly, letting the cart get an inch ahead before she grabbed it again. She was teasing it, making it think she'd let it go, but she wouldn't. She couldn't. Not ever.

Was it worth it?

An answer welled inside her, free for a second, teasing that it might come to her, only to be beaten back by the numbness that almost felt like a natural part of her body now. The music in her ears was the only answer she had:

No, no it's not worth living
But do as you're told
And soon you'll see Harry again

Pete Loam, her mother's boss, held aloft a small box only slightly bigger than the iPod in Siara's pocket. He was a funny guy, always buttoning and unbuttoning his dark jacket, as if never sure what the proper etiquette was. Sometimes he'd leave it unbuttoned as he stood and buttoned as he sat, which Siara thought was backward.

"Inside the vehicle," he said, unbuttoning, "the hydrogen will be stored in these small canisters, making the fuel cell vehicle literally as safe as one powered by gasoline. Safer, if you remember its only emissions are heat and water."

Then he buttoned his jacket again. Buttoned, unbuttoned. You could set your watch by him. Like Sisyphus.

Jeremy Gronson and Harry Keller toppled into each other and rolled in the increasingly chaotic terrain. Jeremy punched, Harry blocked, and even slid in a shot with his left. Jeremy shook it off and came around again with his right, but before he could make contact, Harry kneed him in the gut and seemed to knock the wind out of him.

Pleased though Harry was, he knew he shouldn't be winning a fist fight with Jeremy Gronson. Something was wrong. Out of breath himself, he pulled back, stood, and looked at his opponent.

Harry had learned something about Jeremy while playing chess with him back in school. He settled on a single plan and stuck to it, while Harry sacrificed for position. In a way it was the same as asking questions in exchange for getting hit. Sure, he got pummeled, but he also got information. Even in that chess game, though, sacrificing confused the crap out of Jeremy.

Harry intended his assault as just another way to sacrifice for position, so he was surprised to find himself even briefly with the upper hand. After all, Harry couldn't beat him, just surprise him, piss him off. But now Jeremy was on one knee, huffing, eyes twisted, face turning red, lips white, the opposite of the gaily colored Fool. He clenched his hands into fists, tighter and tighter, his muscles straining so much and his skin turning so red, it looked as if he might drive his fingers through the palms of his own hands. It was like the jock was so angry, he wasn't thinking anymore.

He was losing it.

But was that a good thing or a bad thing, and did it even matter? The event horizon inched toward the tower, which was no longer a simple dark thing. Now it divided reality into polar opposites, sucking out all that remained of the color in the past, mixing it into the blackening future. More fractures formed in the past as the horizon moved, more howls came from the future.

"*Keller!*" Jeremy called. "We're not done."

Back on his feet, he raced at Harry, thudding clumsily on the wobbling ground, as if he were a bear forced to walk upright. Harry stuck his foot out. Jeremy fell for it—he tripped and sprawled forward.

But what good would it do? Jeremy would just keep coming until the school exploded. Harry wasn't even sure why he kept doing it, except maybe in the weird hope that if he made Jeremy mad enough, *he* might explode instead.

How far can I push him? Harry wondered.

Jeremy lunged. Harry moved out of the way again, this time managing to slam Jeremy in the back of the head, sending him down once more.

"How do you do that?" Jeremy screamed. "How?"

"By being willing to get hit," Harry told him, trying to sound all smug and confident. "But I wouldn't expect you to understand. It would be like a dog talking Latin."

Jeremy's nostrils flared. "You mean, like speaking Latin to a dog, moron!"

"Oh yeah? If I'm a moron, why do *you* need herbal tea to get here?"

"Shut up, bag man!"

"*Make* me, tea-bag man!"

Jeremy rose just in time for a new, stronger rumbling to hurl them both off their feet. The cracks in the past were becoming crevices. A large, horrible sound, as if the sky itself had split open, caused them both to turn toward the tower. A wide vertical seam opened in its center. Within it, Harry could make out only a darker dark, but the rush of air and all the colors in the sky now seemed headed toward it.

"Jeremy," Harry said softly. "It looks like something's broken."

"Yeah," Jeremy said. The sound seemed to sober him a little, calm him down. "Guess I should fix that, too. Just as soon as I'm done with you."

Ignoring Harry, he turned back to his path, to do whatever it was he thought would kill Harry. Harry tried following, but the trails were behaving less and less like solid objects and more and more like an angry sea.

Harry was already regretting pissing Jeremy off. He

was, after all, the only one who really knew what was going on with the tower.

"Jeremy!" Harry shouted to him. "Maybe I can wait? Maybe you should fix it now? I promise I won't go anywhere and you can kill me later."

Jeremy paused. "Another sacrifice, Keller?"

Harry watched as he rose up and down on a pulsing trail. The black-robed figure turned toward the tower, then looked back at the spot in the terrain that was his goal. His eyelids fluttered, briefly covering the madness. He thought about it. He shook his head.

"No. We're past that now. I don't care about that thing anymore. I don't care about the Initiation. I don't care about my plans. I don't care about the Masters. Gone, all gone, like dreams. And you know what's left? Just you and me. Just you and my desire to kill you."

He hopped from one wobbly trail to another, finally reaching his goal—Harry's life trail.

"It's been *beyond* annoying dealing with you! It's been cosmic!"

Jeremy wasn't just yelling anymore, he was ripping his voice raw trying to make it rage above the wind and rumbling terrain. He bent down and dug his hands, up to the elbows, into Harry's life.

Harry's brow furrowed. *Is he just going to try to change my trail? Was that his great big idea?*

But then he felt kind of funny, as if something were being yanked from his chest, like his heart and lungs.

170

He looked down at himself. He seemed fine, still just trying to stay on his feet, but then the pain came again, stronger, harder.

He looked at Jeremy. Now he was *really* sorry he'd pissed him off so much. The jock wasn't trying to change things, he was trying to destroy them. He was yanking huge chunks out of Harry's life trail and tossing them onto a growing pile, as if they were garbage. That was his great idea. And it wasn't bad. After all, if that trail was the source of his timeless self, destroying it would destroy Harry completely.

Harry tried to run toward him, but the land was too unmanageable. He fell more than moved.

"Do you know how God created the universe?" Jeremy called.

"With love and kindness?" Harry offered.

"No," Jeremy answered, pulling more and more chunks of trail away. "That's something Chabbers taught me. It was by destroying chaos. By kicking its ass. By beating it into shape. By slamming it down, so that the only thing left was His order."

With that, he dove full-body under Harry's trail.

If Harry felt funny before, now he felt hysterical, like something huge and monstrous was right behind him, ready to swallow him whole. He watched, in utmost horror, as his trail rose, lifted out of the terrain, bowing in the center.

Harry fell. His hands started to shimmy and wobble,

like the water in a pond when you toss in a stone. Dizzy, he tried to keep his focus on his trail. Jeremy was standing under it, lifting it over his head, pushing with those powerful muscles of his. The pressure was starting to make it tear.

Jeremy continued his shredding, yanking huge, oozing hunks out and hurling them this way and that. The more he tore away, the less Harry there was. His hands weren't just wobbling now, they were vanishing, along with his legs and torso. There wasn't much Harry could do about it. Armless, legless, he tried to roll toward Jeremy, but even that was fruitless.

Just as it seemed that the whole world was ready to end, Harry Keller vanished into a whole new nothing.

14. These are the consequences of time.

Before Harry Keller was born, there was an entire eternity of time without Harry Keller, and without which Harry Keller would never have been. But once Harry Keller was born, there Harry Keller was. Once Harry Keller died, of course, there'd be a whole other eternity of time without Harry Keller. While it could be argued that the second entire eternity of time wouldn't be quite the same without there having been a Harry Keller, what could not be argued was the fact that having been born, Harry Keller was, and always would have been.

Yet here there was no time to speak of, no space, no soul, no sight, no sound, no tree to fall, no forest for it to not fall in. Here there wasn't, had not, would not, nor could there be, a Harry Keller, because there was no *had*, no *would*, no *could*.

But there Harry Keller was. Because Harry Keller wasn't dead. Not yet. Not exactly.

How? Maybe he was just an idea now, a reference point, driven by momentum or a memory, the memory of fear, or of love for Siara, or for the ethics his father taught him.

Or maybe he just didn't know when to quit?

Or maybe he had to go on.

Because he couldn't go on.

So he went on.

Am I like Elijah now? I should give her a call. Ask her out for fake coffee. Can I do that without a body? And if I don't have a body, is this what it's like to be dead?

Not knowing many dead, he couldn't tell. In fact, the only dead he really knew were his parents. The moment he thought of them, their faces floated up from the dark.

He'd seen his mother in photos, sensed her in the tremble of his father's voice. But this was the first time he'd just seen *her*, hanging there, moving neither forward nor back. She was as he'd pictured, only more so: passionate, artistic, fiery, but burning so brightly so often, her energies tripped on each other and folded themselves into madness.

His father was next to her. He was no less passionate than his mother, no less insane. His fire was different, as if he were a hunter, using his intellect like a spear. It seemed so strange that such a man believed in something as irrational as God. Maybe he was trying to cover all the angles——before the angels covered him.

Their faces hung there, melting into one another in a way that made Harry feel as though he were looking in a mirror, but that the reflection was more real than he.

No wonder Harry was crazy. He was alive and so was life. What was that poem Mr. Tippicks quoted once, by that guy, E. T. Something?

Mankind cannot bear too much reality.

That was it.

So his parents were human, crazy, and he forgave and loved them for it.

As he did, the faces faded. Like the giant clown said, they were a map, a mask, a filter. With his parent-gods gone, he was alone in zero G, maskless, mapless, feeling no difference between himself and the dark as he hovered above invisible waters. He churned with them, unburdened as they lapped and crashed, their gentle voices of chaos singing sweetly undisturbed.

And then he heard a voice. It wasn't speaking words, ordering the light from the dark, or separating land from sea as if they were quarreling siblings. It wasn't announcing any plan to shape the void and fill it with purpose.

It was just laughing.

It was the same force that had stopped Melody, had made her put down the gun. It was a sad, hearty, serious laugh, a sound that rang though Harry in waves. It shaped the darkness, even though it didn't mean to, in a way that chastened death.

So he laughed with it, realizing it had been so silly to be alive, to have a shape at all, but at the same time, terribly endearing. Now it was easy to let it all go. His fear went, then his love. All desire shivered and faded, washing away the last shimmering borders of self. At the same moment Harry Keller stopped being afraid of life, because it was absurd, he fell hopelessly in love with it, because it was absurd.

The waters shook, the darkness crumbled, and there was light.

He was back in A-Time. And though it felt as if he'd been gone an eternity, he had to admit, it might have been just a moment.

Harry's trail, wounded but no longer being shredded, lay back in its place in the rolling terrain. The pieces torn from it crawled like little Quirks back into it, filling in the gaps.

"Unk! Unk! Unk!" they cried as they worked to make Harry whole.

Jeremy had failed. Something had stopped him. But what? Where was he? Did a Quirk get him? Did his great big tower fall on him?

Harry looked around. No, the tower was still there, deadly as ever, the event horizon minutes away. And there was Jeremy, too.

Seeing him, Harry scrambled to his feet, feeling woozy as the earth continued to tumble beneath him. He felt strongly that Jeremy should also be seeing Harry, but he didn't seem to. He was just standing there in his cool black robes, the wind making them ripple.

"Jeremy?" Harry called.

He didn't answer. There was something wrong with him. Something different about his face. He wasn't angry at all, not anymore. Harry tried to take a few steps closer. Jeremy stood stock-still as the terrain rose and fell around him, as though he were mounted on a wall like a prize fish, or hanging from a string. He looked . . . surprised.

As he neared, Harry could see that Jeremy's head was too high up from his chest. His neck was extended too far. His wide shoulders were slumped. The thick arms twitched slightly, sending small ripples through his robes that Harry had mistakenly thought were caused by the wind. When the trails dove low for an instant, he could see that the tips of Jeremy's feet were floating inches above the ground. He was being held up by something.

Once, when Harry was a boy, he came upon a hawk that had grabbed a squirrel by its shoulders and tried to fly off with it. At first, it seemed like one big creature, half fur and claw, half wing and brown feather. But when Harry saw the look of ultimate surprise in the squirrel's eyes, the knowing that it was about to be food, he realized exactly what was going on.

Jeremy looked like that squirrel.

"Jeremy, what is it? What's going on?"

Harry squinted, trying to make out what was above him. Then he saw it, the scruff of Jeremy's neck pinched between two enormous white-gloved fingers.

The face appeared next—or rather, Harry felt like he was being allowed to see it—the field of white, the red lips, the blue circles around the wide eyes, the forest of orange hair, and the gnashing teeth that now looked hungry.

When the Fool first appeared to Harry, it was a devastating, soul-consuming experience, but in comparison to the face that the archetype revealed now, it had been kind. The creature grinned and spoke.

"Hey, thanks!" it said.

"For what?" Harry asked, hoping it wouldn't hit him again.

"Don't you get it? You got him to give up his plan. As long as he was all about that plan, all about order, I couldn't touch him. But you, you drove him crazy, bit by bit, got him to stop caring about it. There's a thin line between intense order and total chaos. He crossed it, and my dad says I can keep him," the Fool said.

Harry didn't want to know who its dad was; he didn't even know whether to feel proud or disgusted. In either case, Jeremy moaned, then started shrieking. He shrieked so loudly he no longer made words, just vowel sounds punctuated by random consonants. Some sounded like *Keller*, some sounded like *please*, but really, they were meaningless. In them, though, in the tone, Harry could hear Jeremy's mind unpeel.

As Harry watched, the Fool lifted Jeremy higher and higher, up and over his open mouth. Then he began to eat him, bit by bit, peeling off the robes, the arms, the torso.

As the crying, sobbing alpha male's handsome, genetically selected head finally disappeared between the huge gnashing teeth, Harry caught a glimpse of something not so ha-ha in the Fool, something dark and deep. For a brief flash, Harry's gargantuan benefactor didn't look so much like a playful planetary-sized puppy, or even a clown anymore.

He—*it*—looked like the Devil.

Harry shuddered. At the same moment, the Fool's meal disappeared. The bad boy was now in its belly.

A strange quiet ensued. The Fool was still there, as was the tower, as was the deadly storm, but all the shrieking was gone.

He scanned the sky, the future, made black by the tower. It wasn't at all like the darkness Harry had seen when he was dead, or nonextant, or whatever he was. That was peaceful, this malevolent. Colors burst from its ebon hues, but only in flashes that were sucked back into the storm. The event horizon was still moving toward the dark edifice; Siara was still about to toss the banana and blow the school up.

There was still a world to save. Maybe it was just a pretend world, but what the hell.

Harry leapt onto Siara's trail again and tugged at it, but the oozing stuff of the tower had seeped into it, and wherever Harry touched, it burned. He fell backward off the trail, grabbing his hands in agony, and saw the Fool look curiously down at him.

"Can you help?" Harry begged. "Can you stop the chaos?"

The Fool laughed. "Why would I want to do that? I *am* chaos!"

And then, as if their old game of question-and-punch were still in effect, the Fool swatted Harry into the air. When he came back down, he crashed through the surface of the terrain and found himself in something even more familiar.

Harry's eyes snapped open. He was back in the alley a few blocks from school, near where the truck had dropped him off, shivering from the cold and feeling nauseous from the smell of rotting garbage.

It was night. He didn't hear any sirens or large explosions, so he figured there was still time. He raced into the street, pushing his way past shoppers and pedestrians like the madman he was. The funny shoe bags from Windfree slowed him, so he shed them and felt cold asphalt press into his bare feet.

There's a chance, a chance, a chance. . . .

As he approached the corner, a woman wheeling a baby carriage blocked his path. He leapt over the baby, landing in a puddle, almost falling. As he picked up speed again, he heard the woman's outraged cries behind him. He hit the crowded street, barely ducking out of the way of a truck. He heard two cars crash behind him.

But he kept going.

He huffed and puffed, expecting his lungs or legs to give out, but miraculously, neither did. Nothing slowed him in the least until he crossed another street and found himself charging along a long row of department store windows.

He happened to glance inside at what looked like an early Thanksgiving display that seemed more appropriate to a museum than a store. It was too somber, too realistic for the holiday season. Grim Native Americans sat around a roaring campfire. An elder in ceremonial garb reverentially held a small stone between his fingers. On it was a small crude drawing of a coyote. From a tree, an eagle watched, its head twisted sideways. Beyond this scene were distant hills and an evening sky that seemed to go on forever.

Despite its expert realism, Harry wouldn't have given it a second glance had the great bird not jumped off the fake tree, spread its wings, and started flying alongside him.

The window shattered as the bird flew through it. Harry felt a cool wind from the store that smelled of winter coming. He hesitated, but realized he was running out of time and had to keep going. As he did, to his right, he saw, quite clearly, what was once a fake eagle soar high into the city sky. To his left, past the window, he swore he saw the Native Americans move, but it was little more than a fleeting shadow.

A trick. A trick of the light mixing with his panic, he figured. It must be.

Trying to forget it, he kept going until the familiar brick-and-white-stone edge of RAW High School was visible in the distance. Though he thought he could run no faster, he picked up speed until a vast rush and the feeling of something huge and heavy above his shoulders made him turn again to the sky.

Whoa!

This was no bird, real or otherwise. It wasn't even the Fool. A vast white belly, rounded in the center, hovered in the air, with most of the structure unseen beyond it. Though it was a hundred yards straight up, Harry could see rows of rivets in it, indicating that whatever it was, it had been made.

A ship. It was some kind of ship. The sleek metal craft looked as if it had flown straight out of a science-fiction movie, its enormous engines glowing gold as it floated above him, blocking nearly all the stars.

What was it? What was going on? For the first time in his life, Harry knew he wasn't going crazy—the world was. The A-Time storm caused by Jeremy's sculpture was causing the filter of time to unravel completely, bits and pieces of past and future coming loose, popping into the present. Harry staggered as the ship sailed above him.

The one chance, the *only* chance, would be to find the keystone and stop Siara.

Harry lurched forward and ran again. He was on the same block as the school, passing the fenced-in courtyard, heading toward the familiar main entrance, when something large growled. Across the street was another giant, this one of flesh and blood. Taller than the glowing lamps, it stood fifteen to twenty feet high, and, from the tip of its nose to its tail, at least forty feet long.

Its massive jaw had clamped around Mr. Kaufmann's Honda Accord, its teeth ripping through the roof, shattering the glass windows. Harry knew what the large reptilian carnivore was, but even in his mind, he stuttered on the word.

T-t-t-t-t-t-t . . .

Beyond it, on a hill in the field, hooded men pulled on a dozen ropes tied to a great gray rock. Harry had read about the ancient megaliths that had been dug up near the school, but he had no idea who these guys were, and he didn't particularly want to know.

He briefly wondered why the people of the present day weren't reacting to all this, but they seemed not to see, or care. Planning to figure it all out much later, Harry kept running, past the chain-link fence, up the red stone steps, and into the main courtyard. Everything inside was lit up, making the building glow in rich colors.

Beyond the front doors, below the tile mosaic of great thinkers, he could see the auditorium entrance. He flew across the courtyard, feeling concrete, dirt, and sand beneath his feet. The faces of the scientists looked down at him; Einstein, Kepler, Madame Curie, Aristotle. As he ran toward them they grew taller and taller, until they vanished into a line with the sky. Harry threw himself through the doors. He was in the entrance hallway, yards from the auditorium, thrilled to see there was practically no one in the hall. It looked like he had a clear shot.

A saddled, riderless horse galloped across his path, pounding its way toward the social studies department, while a young settler family looked in awe at the bulletin board posters for RAW's high school bands.

It didn't matter. He was here. He'd rush in and grab Siara and everything would tumble back into place. It had to. Without stopping, he headed for the auditorium.

A high-pitched whine grew louder as he stepped in. It was the prototype engine, whirring away on the stage, amplified by the room's acoustics. The place was packed, hundreds of bodies and faces. Whatever madness was going on in the rest of time and space, this room remained untouched. It took Harry a moment to orient himself, but then he saw Siara, wheeling the cart with the deadly banana.

"Siara!" he called. "The banana! You don't know what it's attached to!"

But either the whining engine drowned him out, or she chose not to hear.

He tried to sense the future around him, feel the fastest path to the stage. He could sense nothing in his way, nothing. He could run, jump, and grab the banana. He vaguely remembered the keystone, but there was no more time to look for things he couldn't see. He had to get to her now.

No sooner did he make the decision to run for it then a massive weight pushed him sideways, and someone grabbed him arms.

He hadn't seen them coming at all. They'd arrived, literally, out of nowhere.

"Our old pal, Harry Keller! What a surprise!" a familiar voice said.

"I bet I know who's looking for you!" said another.

Harry whirled and saw his captors; Didi and Gogo, the two school security officers he'd spent so much time ducking and hiding from the last several weeks.

Now, they had to catch him? *Now?*

They tightened their grip on his arms and pulled him toward the exit.

"No!" Harry said, struggling. "Banana! Banana! Banana!"

But beneath the sound of the whining engine it came out more like *babababababababa!*

"Easy. Let's get you some clothes, Ba-ba," Didi said.

"No! No! No!"

It was the keystone. He hadn't found it. What the hell could it be? He looked around frantically, saw a lighter in someone's pocket, a student with a Game Boy, a poster flapping on the wall. People shook hands, made jokes, lifted cans of juice. On stage they flipped switches, read from papers, manipulated a PowerPoint presentation.

It could be anything, anyone, something that hadn't happened, something that had, or one of a million other things he couldn't see or conceive.

And the auditorium clock was about to hit 9 P.M., signaling Siara's deadly snack.

By the time the enormity of the task hit him, the security guards had dragged him into the hallway.

"No!" Harry screamed.

He clawed at their arms, their faces, scratching, punching even biting, but Didi and Gogo were stronger. Having failed to catch Harry on many occasions, tonight they were earning their pay. They hauled him out into the haunted night where giant lizards roamed and dead civilizations rose, somehow oblivious to the temporal carnage around them.

"Don't you see the dinosaur?" he pleaded, pointing.

"Sure, we do, Ba-ba!" Did answered, winking at Gogo as they yanked him across the courtyard. "But it's Barney, the friendly dinosaur!"

It was only then that a sharp, deep noise rattled their chests and made them stop. A microsecond later a concussion wave, a burst of energy from a powerful explosion, hurled all three, Harry, Didi, and Gogo, off the ground and away from each other in what felt like sickly slow motion.

Harry hit the steps with his side, managing to twist toward the school to watch. He was just in time to see all the windows shatter, as if the building were a bursting balloon. Beyond the rain of glass he saw the venerable faces of the great scientists, the ones he'd longed to join, collapse into ten thousand tiny squares, each one a meaningless basic color, purposeless, pointless without the vast context of its million brothers and sisters.

The fireball came next, as if the highlight of a doomsday parade, and it did not disappoint. For its final, burning trick, it turned night into day so quickly that no one had time to scream.

No one, save Harry.

15. A too-late contingent of police cars, fire trucks, and ambulances sped through the city night, their little glowing trails not nearly as bright as the embers of RAW High School. Their sirens wailed, mixing with tire screeches and roaring engines, the sound piercing the urban din. But it, too little and too late, was likewise swallowed by the sound of crackling flames, falling walls, and the hellish rush the bilious smoke made as it poured from the rubble and rose into the circling sky like a vast, upside-down waterfall.

"He knew about the bomb," Didi explained to the barrel-chested police officer who put the cuffs on Harry.

No, officer, it was a banana.

Harry looked at the man as he worked, reading his life at a glance. He was honest but tired, almost a cliché of the good cop. He had two daughters, one high school age, another who would've gone to RAW in a few years. He was two years from retirement, too. He'd make it, but only because his partner would take a bullet for him during a liquor store holdup about six blocks away.

As he worked the cuffs, the cop shook his head. "I've never seen anything like this," he said in a shaky voice.

"He was trying to get into the auditorium, but we stopped him," Gogo put in.

The officer didn't seem to be listening, so both repeated their short story, supporting each other with nods and "yeahs" as they twice told the tale.

When they were done, the burly man asked, "How could anyone do something like this? For what?"

He wasn't looking at Didi or Gogo, he was looking at Harry. His hair was more salt than pepper, and in his hazel eyes was a plea for understanding.

What could Harry say? The truth was pointless.

"Jeremy Gronson wanted to change the past so he could join a transcendental street gang. Only, I guess it didn't work. The dinosaurs, the spaceships, and the Native Americans are gone. Everything seems back to normal."

The cop's face, pink from nearness to the flames, wrinkled in sweaty confusion. Didi and Gogo, who knew Harry, pointed at their temples and swirled their index fingers.

"Cray-zee."

The cop nodded. Harry was nuts. That made sense. Perfect sense. And everything had to make sense. Without any further questions, he grimly shoved Harry into the back of the police car, away from the warmth of the flame, where the cold seat stuck to Harry's naked back.

He leaned forward, peeling his skin off the vinyl interior as the car door slammed. There were no handles on the rear doors, and a metal grate barred him from the front seat.

Of course. This is a police car, I should be used to this sort of thing by now.

But Harry didn't care what they thought, or what they did. The agitated, self-conscious vibration he'd always associated with his madness was silent. He missed it, because it had been such a wonderful buffer against his feelings. But he didn't feel crazy, not anymore, just drained, hollow, full of grief. He didn't blame himself for not spotting the needle in the haystack. He just wished he had.

He even pitied Jeremy, the poor alpha boy Gronson. He'd finally managed to piss on his tree, write his name on reality's wall in a way that would never change, in a way that would ripple out, through the parents of the dead, their friends, their brothers and sisters, altering thousands of lives with waves of trauma and grief. That would be his legacy. His last score. And no one would know.

At least it hadn't been World War III. Harry could sense it in the air, in the fact that the visions of past and future no longer intruded on the urban landscape. Maybe the anachronistic images he'd seen were just the pieces of time Jeremy had built the tower from, or maybe the timeless realms hated a tragedy, or, more likely, even the storm had more to do with the way Harry's mind filtered things than with the things themselves.

But the past *hadn't* changed, so maybe the Fool was wrong, at least about that rule being just a mask. Maybe, really and truly and finally, what was done was done and Nostradamus's prophecy would remain what it had always been—a stupid bunch of words, a not-very-good poem.

Why couldn't it have been a good poem at least?

They drove him to the nearest station, where he was booked and put in a holding cell—yet another room he wasn't allowed to leave. He was thankful it wasn't white, like the lightning that killed his father, or the padded cell at Windfree, or the Fool's gloves, or the flash that took down RAW.

Nope, no whites, just shades of gray. There was a wall of gray bars and in it a door of gray bars. There was gray cinder block, and a gray barred window looking out on a gray parking lot beneath a dark, overcast sky. The only furniture was a bench, painted gray. There wasn't even a cot because probably, he figured, no one would be held here for very long.

But then they told him, "Make yourself comfortable. It'll be a while."

So Harry sat on the gray bench. He tried leaning back against the cold wall until touching it with his back reminded him he didn't have a shirt. They hadn't even given him any clothes, just tossed him in here half naked, shoeless, until someone with mojo could take over the scene.

Maybe they'd try him for the explosion, because he didn't care anymore. Maybe he'd be convicted, but he didn't care anymore. Or maybe, for the hell of it, Harry would show them all what he could do—make a trail of coincidence in A-Time that would shatter all these walls, disarm all their weapons, lay their computer systems low, then calmly walk outside surrounded by his manufactured carnage.

He'd be like the Fool himself then, like a god.

But that would also make him just like Jeremy, wouldn't it?

None of it seemed as funny as it had when he didn't have a body, when he hadn't existed for a while. Now that he was attached to the world again, it all seemed so sad.

Especially Siara.

Harry shivered, leaned forward, looked down at his feet, at the gray floor, and let his feelings go. Tears welled in his eyes, pooled in them, and dripped to the concrete. He rubbed his eyes and looked down at his hands. More tears fell, passing through his palms and hitting the floor where they made small dark wet spots against the gray.

Passing through?

It was true. The tears were passing through his hands, as if he were a ghost. He stuck his index finger against his palm. It went straight through.

What was going on?

Harry snapped his head up. He looked around. He bit his lip and his teeth passed through what should have been the solid flesh of his upper lip. He slammed his hand against the gray paint. It passed through that, too, into the cinder-block wall, out of the wall of the room, and into the A-Time air, where his fingers felt the wind of the still-maddening storm.

When he turned back to the bench, he saw himself sitting there, head buried in hands. The square walls of the cell seemed to curve and melt into A-Time terrain.

He looked to his left and the narrative voice rose:

They drove him to the nearest station, where he was booked and put in a holding cell—yet another room he wasn't allowed to leave. He was thankful it wasn't white, like the lightning that killed his father, or the padded cell at Windfree, or the Fool's gloves, or the flash that took down RAW.

Nope, no whites, just shades of gray. There was a wall of gray bars and in it a door of gray bars. There was gray cinder block, and a gray barred window looking out on a gray parking lot beneath a dark, overcast sky. The only furniture was a bench, painted gray. There wasn't even a cot because probably, he figured, no one would be held here for very long.

But then they told him, "Make yourself comfortable. It'll be a while."

He wasn't in linear time. He was in a life trail. His own. How had that happened? Then he remembered. The Fool had slapped him high into the air. He must have come down in his own trail, in his own future, and mistaken it for the present.

He bolted to his feet and leapt back into the terrain. There the rushing wind nearly knocked him to the ground. The terrain had changed yet again. The past was motionless, flattened out, filled with crevices, drained of all color, making it as gray as his cell. Jeremy's edifice still remained, the center of the vortex. The future, where Harry barely stood, still roiled and wobbled.

The future. What he'd seen hadn't happened yet. Siara hadn't died! Harry had been given a second chance.

A giant in greasepaint with teeth that could crack the world like an egg laughed from inside him, from a deeper place than the Quirk-shard ever occupied.

Good one, huh? You should see the look on your face! If I had a camera, I'd take a picture.

Harry shook his head in disbelief. So it was a practice

run. If he'd done things differently, the school would not have exploded. But what had he done wrong?

The keystone. He hadn't found the keystone.

"What is it?" he shouted. "What?"

But the Fool wasn't answering, and the ground only rumbled in response. The spot where Harry stood rose and fell with abandon, as if it had never wanted to be still in the first place. The event horizon, unperturbed by any shift in the A-Time weather, hissed closer to the end.

The world, this world anyway, wasn't going to tell him a damn thing.

Or maybe it was, maybe it'd been telling him all along, telling him everything he needed to know. It was, after all, the world. He just didn't know how to read it.

But what could he read? Terrain, trails—they yielded their secrets fast enough.

He looked at the imposing black column that divided time. It was made of terrain, so the answer was somewhere in there. Whatever the keystone was had to be spelled out inside the column. If Harry could get in, the events would rise in images, and he could follow the path of events back to the keystone.

He struggled across the churning trails. As he approached the tower, he felt something akin to heat radiate from its ebon surface. It burned his hand as he touched it. Didn't just burn it, he noticed when he looked, but melted it clean away to the wrist.

Harry stepped back, howling, staring at the stub at the end of his arm. In seconds, his hand re-formed.

Jeremy said it was built to funnel timeless energy, ergon, so it's probably sucking energy from me, too. Only, since I'm generated by my trail, it can't suck me dry. Even if my ergon burned up completely, I'd probably just wind up back in linear time.

He eyed the tower, tried to gauge how much it would hurt if he forced himself inside, and wondered if he could stay conscious long enough to see the keystone.

Another sacrifice for position. Worth a shot.

Harry ran at it, pushing into the ooze with his shoulder. As his body hissed and melted, he tried to ignore the pain.

Eahhjjj!

He stumbled back in anguish, looking like a piece of ice, half-melted against a burning grill. When he saw to his horror how much of him was gone, he realized he wasn't strong enough or fast enough to pull this off.

He knew from physics that force was equal to mass times acceleration, meaning that if you could get a blade of grass to move fast enough, it could bury itself in a thick piece of oak. But how could Harry ever achieve that kind of speed? He wasn't a god, he was a Harry Keller. At this point, he was just three quarters of a Harry Keller.

The Fool's words came back to him:

Points of entry are arbitrary. Let reason go, pick a partner, and dance.

Let reason go. How could he do that, with maybe a minute left to save the school? Or was that his problem yet again? Had he just been thinking, rationalizing too much? Clicking his teeth impatiently, he tried to stop thinking and let ideas just rise to his mind. . . .

Alligator, alligator, hump-backed whale . . .

(didn't make any sense but he loved it)

That ride's over, want another?

(he shivered at the memory)

The sidewalk was moving. Not just moving, undulating, waving in patterns that made the asphalt crack and tear. It was just like a film he'd seen in physics of the Tacoma Narrows Bridge in 1940.

(Where the heck was that from?)

Oh yeah. Part of the visions he'd had right before he first entered A-Time. The image, newly conjured now, stuck with him. Wobbling bridge. Vibrations. Resonance. Wind made the bridge wobble like a wave, until the energy built up so much that it collapsed. Solid ground acting like the sea.

He looked at the rambling future terrain. It certainly had enough waves in it, but they were all over the place. It looked like a many-headed snake that, for the life of it, couldn't decide on a single direction. A lot of power there, though, a lot of energy, if he could figure out how to direct it.

Like the Tacoma Narrows Bridge.

Could he? Bounce on a few trails in just the right spot, set up a resonance, send a wave in the right direction and ride it, like a surfer, toward the tower? If the momentum was strong enough, he might be able to use it to burst inside and melt in its mouth, not in its hands.

Why not?

Well, there were a million reasons, but reason hadn't worked so far, so Harry put each foot on a wobbling trail and started pumping. After a second, like a bucking horse, the trails threw him. He flopped backwards onto a third writhing trail, wrapped his arms around it to get his balance back, and finally stood on its top.

Then he rode it, bending as it went down, straightening as it went up. It was like playing on a swing in his elementary schoolyard, pumping, making it swing like a pendulum: higher, higher, higher, lower, lower, lower, but all the time, faster. Soon the whole trail was practically leaping out of the terrain.

The energy in the bucking trail was soon as high as Harry could make it and still stay on. As it crested a final time, Harry leapt toward the tower. He flew into it, as if hurled by a slingshot.

Some days you're the windshield, some days you're the bug.

But even a bug, if thrown hard enough, can crack a windshield. Which is exactly what Harry did, his head and body making a horrible sound as they penetrated the sickly ooze.

He was in. The pain was ridiculous, like being stabbed by a thousand needles, a million paper cuts, like being bitten by a thousand snakes, being burned alive, inside and out, or having acid shoot through all your veins at once. His legs were gone already, so were his hands, but all he really needed were his eyes and ears. As his A-Time form boiled and melted, he scanned the ugly black walls.

The scene he'd seen play out in Siara's future rose before him, only this time, golden strands clung to the events, tying them to the rest of the tower.

It was 7:59, and the second hand swept toward twelve. The minute hand shivered and clicked into place. Eight o'clock. It was time.

She peeled the banana, took a bite, and started chewing. Most of the crowd was still applauding, but a few saw her eating and laughed. Her mother turned from the crowd, the smile fading from her face.

"Siara," she whispered. "What are you doing?"

"Siara!" her father hissed from the front row. "Get down! What is wrong with you?"

But her mouth was full, so she didn't answer.

More and more of the crowd were watching, not the engine, but her. Dree, Jasmine, and Hutch looked worried. Her mother looked frozen with shame. Her father was furious.

He leapt out of his seat and came up the side stairs. "Siara, stop this nonsense immediately!"

At about the same time, Pete Loam also saw her. He unbuttoned his jacket and came at her from the opposite direction.

"Excuse me, Miss."

She was done eating. All that was left was the peel. She reached out and dropped it just in time for her father to step on it. He flew forward, slamming Pete Loam in the chest.

Loam's open jacket flared on either side of him, making him look like he had small but well-tailored wings as he sailed backward into the whirring engine. There were chugs and sparks as he hit. Tubes came loose and flew about like raging spaghetti.

Siara's father was just getting up, nose bloodied, when a single spark hit the end of one of the small canisters, igniting the hydrogen in it, and sending it sailing like a guided missile into the heart of the huge hydrogen tank.

Harry, barely a skull, spotted what he needed: a golden line, barely visible, connecting one event directly to the explosion. Scanning backward, he followed it back to its source:

.knat negordyh eguh eht fo traeh eht otni elissim dediug
a ekil gnilias ti gnidnes dna ,ti ni negordyh eht gnitingi
,sretsinac llams eht fo eno fo dne eht tih kraps elgnis a
nehw ,deidoolb eson ,pu gnitteg tsuj saw rehtaf s'araiS
.ittehgaps gnigar ekil tuoba welf dna esool emac sebuT
.tih eh sa skraps dna sguhc erew erehT .enigne gnirrihw

eht otni drawkcab delias eh sa sgniw deroliat-llew tub

llams dah eh ekil kool mih gnikam ,mih fo edis rehtie

no deralf tekcaj nepo s'maoL

.tsehc eht ni maoL eteP gnimmals ,drawrof welf eH .ti no pets

ot rehtaf reh rof emit ni tsuj ti deppord dna tuo dehcaer ehS

.leep eht saw tfel saw taht llA .gnitae enod saw ehS

".ssiM ,em esucxE"

.noitcerid etisoppo eht morf reh ta emac dna tekcaj sih

denottubnu eH .reh was osla maoL eteP ,emit emas eht

tuoba tA

"!yletaidemmi esnesnon siht pots ,araiS" .sriats edis eht

pu emac dna taes sih fo tuo tpael eH

.suoiruf saw rehtaf reH .emahs htiw nezorf dekool

rehtom reH .deirrow dekool hctuH dna ,enimsaJ ,eerD

.reh tub ,enigne eht ton ,gnihctaw erew dworc eht fo

erom dna eroM

.rewsna t'ndid ehs os ,lluf saw htuom reh tuB

"?uoy htiw gnorw si tahW !nwod teG" .wor tnorf eht

morf dessih rehtaf reh "!araiS"

"?gniod uoy era tahW" .derepsihw ehs ",araiS"

.ecaf reh morf gnidaf elims eht ,dworc eht morf denrut

rehtom reH .dehgual dna gnitae reh was wef a tub

,gnidualppa llits saw dworc eht fo tsoM .gniwehc detrats

dna ,etib a koot ,ananab eht deleep ehS

.emit saw tI .kcolc'o thgiE .ecalp otni dekcilc dna dere-

vihs dnah etunim ehT .evlewt drawot tpews dnah dno-

ces eht dna ,95:7 saw tI

There it was, right there. It was so obvious. Simple.

Elegant. Too smart for the crass football player. Harry had to wonder if it was Siara's influence that gave Jeremy the idea

As soon as he saw what he needed to see, Harry let the burning take what was left of him, his head, ears, and eyes. Having made the final sacrifice, having destroyed himself yet again, he found himself returning home, as he'd guessed, to linear time.

Siara was on the stage, now near the curtain's edge. She looked at the clock, remembering the one Harry was stuck on before he fell, remembering the poem she'd written about Sisyphus as the minute hand, pushing up in one direction, falling back down, forever, carrying not rocks but the burden of time.

It was 7:59, and the second hand swept. The minute hand shivered . . .

. . . and collapsed back into place. It was still 7:59.

It shivered again but again didn't reach the twelve. It just sat there, shivering, waiting, as if for once Sisyphus had said to himself, "Screw it, I'm not taking another damn step."

Siara stared.

And for some reason, despite the singing voice insisting she should do as she was told, she smiled, nodded, and, with a mouth full of banana said, "Screw it. I'm not taking another damn step."

16. As Harry Keller burst into the auditorium and saw Siara, he figured he wasn't done just yet. He thought he'd have to barrel into her and wrestle the peel from her hands before someone stopped him.

He didn't, though.

The instant Siara laid eyes on his shirtless, insane form rushing down the aisle, leaping gracefully over some obstacles, tripping awkwardly over others, she cried out, "Harry!" and yanked the iPod earbuds out.

Harry felt a wave of vertigo pass through him. He didn't see it, not exactly, but he felt the vast structure in A-time, the grotesque thing Jeremy had worked so hard on for so long, crash and crumble into pieces so small that whatever remained was swept away by the time trails as they rolled and shifted back into place atop it.

It was over. Really over.

Sorta.

Having heard Siara's screams, the auditorium fell

silent. Despite the whirring and the lights up on stage, all eyes were on Harry and Siara as they raced toward each other. A few yards to go, Siara, wanting to free her hands, tossed the banana peel. It landed a few feet in front of Harry. He, of course, slipped on it and fell into her, nearly knocking her over. But then she hugged him so tightly she literally squeezed the air out of him.

"You're alive! You're alive! You're alive!" she screamed, burying her head in his shoulder.

Harry could only smile and gasp. "Yeah, I guess I am."

"When time stopped, I knew it was you. I knew it."

Harry shrugged. "Well, I didn't stop time. It was just a piece in the clock. I made it wear out a little sooner than it was supposed to. It was part of something called a keystone, but I can explain that later."

Their eyes met. He could see how totally happy she was to see him and wondered if she knew the feeling was mutual. A pleasant tingling ran over his senses, the first nice and gentle thing that had made his head swim in ages.

So is this finally the part where I get the girl?

The auditorium doors burst open. Didi and Gogo appeared. If that weren't enough, Siara's mother and father were climbing down from the stage, not looking very happy. Soon all three men were in the aisle, coming up fast from either side.

Harry knew they'd pull him away in a few seconds, but there was something he needed to do first. He moved his head forward; Siara moved hers. Their lips were a fraction of an inch apart. He inhaled the sweet breath she exhaled, and they kissed.

Feeling vaguely embarrassed by the intense silence that had filled the auditorium, he pulled gently away. "Siara . . . um . . . everyone . . . and your parents . . ."

But Siara didn't seem to care much.

"You're alive," she said. "How are you alive?"

"Long story," he said, but before he could start it, she kissed him again.

This is great, Harry thought, kissing back. *And I'm not even being yanked into A-Time.*

But then he heard Siara's parents storming up, Didi and Gogo racing toward him.

"That's my daughter!"

"Let the girl go, Keller!"

Even so, they kept kissing, and the moment seemed to last forever.

But when forever finally ended, it wasn't because Didi or Gogo grabbed Harry, or because Mr. and Mrs. Warner pulled Siara away. Nope. Before anyone's harsh hand could touch either of them, something yanked Harry Keller out of his body and pulled him into A-Time.

Not now! he thought.

As Harry's body began to collapse, he saw Siara's beautiful eyes widen in surprise. Then she unfurled into her trail, along with the rest of time. And there he was again.

At least the storm was gone. Quirks, Glitches, and Timeflys once again dotted the terrain. As Harry had sensed, the huge edifice that scarred the landscape had vanished. Everything was as it had been the very first time he entered the nonlinear realm.

He should have been satisfied, but he was more annoyed.

He stomped his feet and yelled at A-Time. "Bad A-Time! *Bad!* What is it *now*? Can't I get a single fricking break here?"

A small Quirk "unked!" as it dodged Harry's stomping. He kicked at the ground behind it, narrowly missing its lobster-size claws as it fled. "Was it you? Are you some drag-poor-Harry-into-A-Time-just-as-he's-getting-the-girl Quirk?"

He was clenching his fists when he noticed his hands and arms glowing. The radiance wasn't from some inner light. It was from something outside. He looked up. The source was easy enough to spot. A bright light shone from a golden pinprick in the multicolored sky. The funny star swelled so brightly, Harry had to shield his eyes. It tore itself free and drifted to the ground a few yards away.

What is this? The Wizard of Oz? *I hope I don't have to wear ruby slippers. . . .*

Harry squinted—the light was nearly blinding, but

at its center he could make out the figure of a man. When the sphere landed, the man stepped out of the light, and in an instant, Harry knew who it was.

"Mr. Tippicks?" Harry said.

"Yes, Harry," Emeril Tippicks said. "It's me."

A feeling of guilt slammed Harry. "I, like, totally forgot all about you! I'm so sorry! Are you okay?"

Tippicks's smile widened, like that of a man who'd found God right where he left Him. "Couldn't be better, Mr. Keller, couldn't be better. You see, I met my dead father. Saw him, spoke to him. He's still . . . well, maybe not alive—it's more accurate to say he still exists here. All the little accidents I had today—well, turns out they weren't accidents. It was him, sort of tapping me on the shoulder, trying to let me know he was here. For years, I thought he'd died, but he'd simply chosen to become something else. He's one of the Obscure Masters. And now I've had a chance to say how sorry I was to have doubted him. I have so much to thank you for, so very much, Mr. Keller."

He extended his hand. Harry reached out to shake it and smiled politely, but he was really thinking, *That's all great, but it's your happy ending. Can I get back to Siara now?*

Still, having abandoned his teacher in A-Time, he felt obliged to make small talk. "So . . . glad none of us are crazy and all of us are alive, huh? So to speak, I mean. Are you . . . uh . . . planning to stay?"

Tippicks shook his head. "No, no. Can't, really. Apparently I have some part to play in something the Masters are working on. Very hush-hush."

"Cool," Harry said. "Hey, any chance you'll recommend me for regular classes now? I mean, assuming I can stay out of Windfree?"

"Oh. As I understand it, you'll stay out. The Masters said they're already arranging that and you shouldn't worry, but that you could fix it all just as easily yourself. They told me a few things, and I'm afraid I didn't understand everything they said. As for the classes, if it makes any difference, I'll be happy to make the recommendation."

"Great, and I'm glad the uh . . . Masters aren't angry with me for messing up their boy's Initiation," Harry said. "They do seem to have a kind of lax attitude toward, you know, human life."

"Well, I'd have to say that they definitely didn't seem as worried about it as you or I might be, but my impression is that they're not so bad. Some of them are even immortalized on the mosaic in front of our school. And you see, Harry, that's why I'm here. They wanted me to tell you something, something they're surprised you haven't figured out yourself yet."

"What? Did someone leave a sweater at the giant edifice thing?"

"No. The Initiation, Harry. It was never Jeremy's. It was yours."

"Mine?" Harry said.

Tippicks nodded. "That's what they said. They've been watching you from the beginning. And you passed. The word *splendidly* was used. Now they want you to join their ranks. They want to teach you all they've discovered. They wanted me to tell you that the Fool is only the first of the archetypes, and even the archetypes are just the beginning, not that I have any idea what that means. They want you to know it won't be all fun and games. There's a lot of hard work, terribly hard. You'll have to stay here most of the time, even after death, but if what I saw is any indication, the rewards are beyond compare—and I don't mean the money. I've seen them Harry. It's like they're a whole other race unto themselves. The next step up."

When Harry didn't answer right away, Tippicks grinned. "It's your decision of course, but if you ask my advice, I have to tell you, I've reviewed a lot of colleges for my students, and this a pretty sweet deal."

Harry stood there open-mouthed, thinking of all he'd been through, all he'd seen, and about how much more he wanted to see, how many more questions he wanted answered, whether they made sense or not. It had been such a long walk from when he first arrived and believed he was like Columbus, the first to land on the A-Time shores. Then again, the Native Americans were in North America before Columbus. And they say the Norse arrived before him, too, and maybe the Irish, and the Romans, and the Chinese. And who knows who else?

"What do you say?" Tippicks asked.

Harry closed his mouth and twisted his head. "No."

Tippicks frowned. "No?"

Harry nodded. "No."

Tippicks sighed. "Nostradamus will be disappointed, but not surprised. I have to confess, though, *I'm* surprised. Would you mind if I asked why?"

Harry shrugged. "Well, remember how you were teaching us the *Odyssey* in Special-Ed class? You know the part where Odysseus visits the land of the dead, and on the way back out, his guide takes him to two doors? One leads to reality, and the other leads to the land of dreams and shadows. Odysseus is about to take the door to reality, but his guide stops him and says no. He points him at the door that leads to the realm of dreams. 'That's *your* world, he explains.' So, I guess I just feel the same way. It's my world."

Tippicks thought about it a moment, then nodded. "It's like TS Eliot said, *Mankind cannot bear too much reality.*"

Harry furrowed his brow. "Did you ever quote him to me before?"

"Not that I remember. Why?"

"Never mind."

"Well," Tippicks said, still smiling. "I was told it would be rude to try to change your mind, but there is one more thing before I send you back to deal with Ms.

Warner and her parents. The Masters realize it's your nature to be terribly curious, so, given all they've put you through, I'm empowered to answer one question. No gods will hit you. Whatever question you like will be answered in quick and simple terms with no repercussions whatsoever."

Harry thought a moment. *I stopped a suicide, a mass shooting, dated myself, and got totally deconstructed. I found out linear time doesn't exist and that the borders of the human self are more an opinion than a fact. What else would I like to know?*

A few Timeflys flitted about in the sky above him, reflecting colors off their ephemeral skin. Harry smiled at the sight of them.

"What *are* those?" he asked.

Tippicks looked up. He twisted his head sideways as if he were listening to something, then spoke. "Those? Those are dreamers. Everyone comes to A-Time when they're asleep. They just don't remember." He turned to look at Harry. "I'm told it will be like that for me when I return. I won't remember seeing my father. The Masters have their secrets to keep, but I was promised I will always remember what it felt like."

Harry was about to ask how Tippicks would be able to keep his word on helping him get back into class if he didn't remember, but before he could say anything, Tippicks shifted in the air. His balding head moved down to the center of his body as his arms and legs folded in.

For a second, Harry thought it was like when Elijah vanished, but Tippicks wasn't disappearing; he was changing. Colors came forth in patterns as his body squared. His face melted into the flatness.

"Initiation is awakening Harry. Try not to nod off."

Tippicks undulated a few times, as if testing his new form, then flew away to join the other Timeflys that dove, wove, and spun in the timeless rainbow sky.

"Well look at that, would you?" Harry said.

Then he got back to Siara, her parents, and the world.

Epilogue

Pushing the present
From six until twelve
Sisyphus times his own prison

He can't hear the ticking
He's too busy kicking
Dead in the center, just spinning

Then he falls just as slow
But it's not far to go
When you have to end up beginning

—SIARA WARNER, TENTH GRADE

As Jeremy stepped through, a trophy appeared in his arms. It felt warm, like the hug of a mother; perfect, like a father's approval.

He wasn't sure where he was, but he knew he'd won. Harry Keller was as dead.

And now the kisses of a hundred gorgeous women awaited him and the balm of sweet water that poured from a hundred fountains not built by the hand of man.

His smile faded when he saw there was one last door, beyond which lay an even greater prize.

So he ran to it, not noticing the trophy in his hands vanishing. He pushed the door and it yielded, like a woman who wanted him in the worst possible way.

And there at last was the final, dizzying truth.

As Jeremy stepped through, a trophy appeared in his arms. It felt warm, like the hug of a mother; perfect, like a father's approval.

He wasn't sure where he was, but he knew he'd won. Harry Keller was as dead.

And now he kisses of a hundred gorgeous women awaited and the balm of sweet water that poured from a hundred fountains not built by the hand of man.

His smile faded when he saw there was one last door, beyond which lay an even greater prize.

So he ran to it, not noticing the trophy in his hands vanished. He pushed the door and it yielded, like a woman who wanted him in the worst possible way.

And there at last was the final, dizzying truth.

As Jeremy stepped through, a trophy appeared in his arms. It felt warm, like the hug of a mother; perfect, like a father's approval.

He wasn't sure where he was, but he knew he'd won. Harry Keller was as dead.

And now he kisses of a hundred gorgeous women awaited and the balm of sweet water that poured from a hundred fountains not built by the hand of man.

His smile faded when he saw there was one last door, beyond which lay an even greater prize.

So he ran to it, not noticing the trophy in his hands vanished. He pushed the door and it yielded, like a woman who wanted him in the worst possible way.

And there at last was the final, dizzying truth.

As Jeremy stepped through, a trophy appeared in his arms. It felt warm, like the hug of a mother; perfect, like a father's approval.

He wasn't sure where he was, but he knew he'd won. Harry Keller was as dead.

And now he kisses of a hundred gorgeous women awaited and the balm of sweet water that poured from a hundred fountains not built by the hand of man.

His smile faded when he saw there was one last door, beyond which lay an even greater prize.

So he ran to it, not noticing the trophy in his hands vanished. He pushed the door and it yielded, like a woman who wanted him in the worst possible way.

And there at last was the final, dizzying truth.

As Jeremy stepped through, a trophy appeared in his arms. It felt warm, like the hug of a mother; perfect, like a father's approval.

He wasn't sure where he was, but he knew he'd won. Harry Keller was as dead.

And now he kisses of a hundred gorgeous women awaited and the balm of sweet water that poured from a hundred fountains not built by the hand of man.

His smile faded when he saw there was one last door, beyond which lay an even greater prize.

So he ran to it, not noticing the trophy in his hands vanished. He pushed the door and it yielded, like a woman who wanted him in the worst possible way.

And there at last was the final, dizzying truth . . .

"Time is speeding up. And to what end? Maybe we were told that two thousand years ago. Or maybe it wasn't really that long ago; maybe it is a delusion that so much time has passed. Maybe it was a week ago, or even earlier today. Perhaps time is not only speeding up; perhaps, in addition, it is going to end.

And if it does, the rides at Disneyland are never going to be the same again. Because when time ends, the birds and hippos and lions and deer at Disneyland will no longer be simulations, and, for the first time, a real bird will sing."

—PHILIP K. DICK, 1978

Acknowledgments

Again and always to Liesa Abrams for rescuing *Squalor* from timeless obscurity. To Eloise Flood for agreeing with her. To Margaret Wright for putting up with my flailings and failings, and the same to Amy Stout-Moran, wherever she may be. To Andy Ball and Ben Schrank for picking up where others left off.

To Who Wants Cake (Dan Braum, K. Z. Perry, Lee Thomas, Nick Kaufmann, and Sarah Langan—the best crit group *ever!*) not only for their advice, but also just for seeming happy whenever they got to read another chapter of Harry and Co. Now that I'm out of NY and living in Amherst, I shall miss these scarecrows most of all.

Lastly, since all selves may be fictional, to Harry Keller, my first profesional fictional creation, named not after some latter-day boy wizard, but after poor, crazed Harry Haller (from Herman Hesse's *Steppenwolf*) and Helen Keller, whose lack of sight and hearing gave her glimpses of a greater world. Hope I did right by you!